Published
www.in.

M000203950

ISBN (eBook): 978-1-915275-91-2
ISBN (Paperback): 978-1-915275-92-9
ISBN (Hardback): 978-1-915275-93-6

Bridie,

4th Oct 20..

INTO THE WOODS

LORRAINE MURPHY

Best wishes

Lorraine Murphy

INKUBATOR
BOOKS

PROLOGUE

I tiptoe through the darkness, trying not to make a noise, counting my steps in my inside voice – right three, forward two, left five. I can't lose concentration, trip on a twig or stumble on a rock. I try to remember the story of Snow White.

"What would you do?" Mammy asked, tucking me into my pink bed after my bedtime story. "If you were Snow White, and the huntsman brought you into the woods to kill you?"

"Easy peasy. Daddy would come and save me."

Mammy tutted and made a big breath. "Always Daddy. And if Daddy was away at work, what would you do then?"

"I'd run and hide."

Now, here in the woods, I can't run. I can't see her or her gun, but I know she is there.

"Scarlett, I'm not going to hurt you. I love you. Come out, come out, wherever you are." I freeze. She's very close.

"Ah, there you are," she says.

1

KAREN

Day 1 – 17:55

Five minutes to the most important meeting of my life. I launch Zoom on the office PC and enable the webcam. The evening sun shines on the grey walls, making a picture-perfect backdrop to the vase of sunflowers on the white bookshelf. I select the book with the pink cover and leave it on my desk, ready to discuss it with its celebrated author. A portrait of the three of us hangs above the bookshelf. Paddy, Scarlett and me. All smiles.

I catch a glimpse of myself on-screen. Holy mother, I look wrecked. With no time to do anything except fake it, I set the halo light behind the screen to amber, increase the Zoom touch-up level and play with the camera settings until my creases have all but disappeared. A tractor roars in the field outside our renovated farmhouse, drowning out the evening birdsong. It will be difficult to hear, but it's far too hot to close the small sash window. I toggle the camera to the right, and black and white cattle grazing on the lush green fields come into view.

I still can't believe Dr Goldberg, US child psychologist and darling of the chat show circuit, is coming to Ireland for me. As a long-time blogger, some of my previous videos hit over 1K views, but that was before, and this is on a different level. The day I uploaded that video sharing my struggles, I expected nothing to come from it, but it hit the zeitgeist, and within days, I was on national TV, and the video went viral. It was an incredible experience, but the backlash – that was brutal. Trolling, nasty comments, threats, but worse than that – I was cancelled. All my hard work undone overnight. Many said my honesty and openness helped them at first, but as the fury grew, they fell away. I would give anything to undo it all up until the point where Dr Goldberg contacted me, calling the interview "the most honest and important piece of our time."

She emailed, saying: "It is a rare thing for a mother to talk with brutal honesty about her struggles. I take my hat off to you." I replied, thanking her, and invited her to do an online seminar for parents in Ireland, which, to my disbelief, she agreed to. This is my shot at redemption, my chance to regain my reputation.

Everything was in hand until last week when she decided to come to Ireland in person if I could "make that happen." She wanted to keep her original online date and add a couple more to it. My mother always told me to be fierce, be brave and go after what I want, and that's what I did. Since then, I've been flat out developing new skills – event management, travel consultant, ticket seller, marketing and public relations, all the time terrified I'll be unmasked as the fraud that I am. I could have imposter syndrome, or maybe I haven't been honest about my skill set. My ancient phone is hot from deleting and adding apps.

Even with all this effort, I haven't found accommodation for her visit next weekend, which coincides with Ireland playing England in the rugby. Every decent place in Dublin is booked, and there is no room at the inn for the Goddess Goldberg, it seems, who insists on a five-star minimum.

An alert pops up on my computer screen.

Meeting with Dr Goldberg starting now.

Last check. My fitted blue shirt is formal, my denim shorts and flip-flops out of shot. I tie my long blonde hair into a loose bun at the nape of my neck and clear my desk – papers, books and the mug from last night.

"Peace offering," Paddy said when he brought me tea last night, long after Scarlett had gone to sleep. He bent to kiss me on the cheek, then hesitated before kissing me on the lips. "Is this okay?"

"Yes, it's okay." He was trying, and it would be wrong to say otherwise, but he was awkward, forced. We both were. I continued to type while Paddy sipped his tea behind me.

"What are you working on?" he asked.

"Preparing for tomorrow's meeting with Dr Goldberg. Still no joy in finding a hotel. She wants five-star standard."

He tapped his iPhone, and my old smartphone beeped. "I've sent you the ICT Travel app we use for our top visiting clients. Mention you're married to the senior partner Paddy O'Hara. That should swing it for you."

"Thanks, but I am running out of hope. The rugby is on next weekend."

"Oh, that's right." He ran his hands through his short brown hair, now greying at the sides. "I've tickets for that game."

"She might have to stay here, yet."

He chuckled. "You're joking."

"I am. So far."

He yawned and broke into a stretch. "I'm wrecked."

"Go to bed."

"I'd love to, but I've to pack for London. Have to be out of here in six hours. Early meeting before work. No rest for the wicked."

He would be gone until Monday, three days off from working on our marriage. I let him massage my shoulders, and the tension eased.

"Come to bed," he breathed into my ear, and my shoulders tightened again. I forced a smile. "In a while, you go ahead."

He kissed my cheek. "Don't be too long. I'll say goodnight to Scarlett..."

"Don't you dare – she's fast asleep, and I have too much work to do to have her up. I'll tell her you said goodnight when she wakes up in the morning."

It was hours later when I slipped under the blankets beside him, his chest rising and falling in a deep sleep. When I woke this morning, he was gone. I starfished in the bed and dreamed of having it to myself for three more glorious nights. Three nights of not walking on eggshells.

Another alert pops up on my screen. Dr Goldberg is waiting to be admitted to the meeting. I push back my shoulders, paint on a smile and click Start Meeting.

Silver-haired, with blood-red lipstick and winged glasses, the sexagenarian smiles, and the enormity of the situation hits me like a steam train. Dr Goldberg!

"Good afternoon, or should I say good evening," she greets me in a New York accent.

"Good afternoon, Dr Goldberg. I'm so excited about this meeting. Thank you for joining me."

"A pleasure." She leans into her camera. "Oh, that's a pretty place you have."

I glance over my shoulder at the scene outside my window. It is beautiful. I'm glad we moved. "It's County Westmeath in the midlands. We're new here, but I do love it. It's very peaceful."

"I can see why; it looks stunning. It's always been a dream of mine to come over to Ireland and, oh, I'm super-stoked to make it come true next week."

"Have you family here?" I already know the answer from my extensive research.

Her eyes light up. "Oh yes. We go back three generations on my mother's side. My great-grandmother came over from County Cork."

I love how animated she is when she talks about her granny, which she does at length. Irish people emigrated to the four corners of the earth, but their ancestors never forgot who they were and where they originated. I imagine her grandmother, shawled and emaciated, boarding a coffin ship during the Great Famine in search of a better life. I can see her looking down with immense pride on her granddaughter. It makes me emotional that being Irish, being one of us, makes her happy.

I hold up the pink book, *Fairy Tales: A Theory of Mind over Matter*, and she stops talking. "Dr Goldberg, this book is a masterpiece."

"You're too kind. I have always found fairy tales a superb way to teach our children."

She launches into a spiel about her childhood and the role fairy tales played in it. It's fascinating, but too much time has passed, and I need to veer this conversation back to business. "It's still number one in Ireland."

She beams.

"Four weeks in a row," I add. *Ping*, an email notification from the Dromod Hotel.

Half afraid to hope, I open it.

Dear Guest... enquiry... good news... cancellation... room
available on dates requested.

"Am I keeping you from more important things, dear?"
the doctor asks, her smile unfaltering but no longer reaching
her eyes.

"The Dromod Hotel in Killiney has a room for you," I say,
wanting to scream my head off but maintaining a professional tone.

She joins her fingers at the tips. "I thought everything was
in hand."

Did I tell her that?

"Oh, it was, but this is an upgrade. It's a mediaeval castle
in Dublin Bay, overlooking Dublin Bay and the Irish Sea.
You're going to love it."

When the corners of her mouth turn up, I know I'm off
the hook. Relief and excitement flood through me in equal
measure. I glance back at the notification.

Click this link if you wish to book without delay.

"Can we take a brief break while I make the booking?" I
ask. "It would be a shame to miss this opportunity."

With her blessing, I end the call and follow the link. Holy
crap, it's €350 per night, paid in advance, and way more than I
expected. That's a lot, considering I have no income, but what
can I do? It's the only suitable place available, and the doctor
is waiving her usual €5K-a-day speaking fee. I click Pay Now,
hoping that Paddy isn't asked to confirm the card purchase,
and try to ignore the total for the three nights the doctor
requested.

At least the City Conference Centre will accept payment
on the day; ticket sales should cover that cost. If the online
interest translates to real-life bums on seats, sales might cover

the Dromod too, but if it doesn't... so much rests on the success of this event. I should check with Paddy before putting such a large purchase on his credit card, but he's away to London, and this can't wait. I might not recoup it all, but he's a senior partner with ICT Technologies and minted – he'll get over it.

With the last piece of the puzzle in place, the adrenaline kicks in, and I give myself a virtual pat on the back. It's been a nightmare, a massive challenge, but I did it. I organised this whole conference myself.

The front door opens and closes downstairs. I'm not expecting anyone. I stop typing and listen out, but there is silence. Then a footstep on the stairs. And another.

There is someone in my house. My heart thumps as the footsteps get louder and closer, coming towards me, and when a man passes my study, I scream from the pit of my stomach.

He staggers backwards, clutching his chest. "Karen, what the fuck?"

"Paddy? What... what are you doing? Are you trying to kill me?"

He holds on to the white banisters and pants. "You nearly gave me a heart attack."

The sweat is pouring off me. "I nearly gave YOU a heart attack? What about me? Why didn't you call out when you came in?"

He wipes his red face on his white shirt. "Didn't... mean... to startle you."

He comes towards me, but I put my hands up for him to stay away. "I need a minute; you really scared me. I thought you were an intruder."

"The house was quiet when I came in... I thought you guys were outside."

"You're not supposed to be here. Why are you here?"

"London was cancelled. The client didn't sign the contract. I was miles away, thinking about going for a swim, and you pounced, gave me the fright of my life."

I slide his credit card under the pink book. Disappointment rapidly replaces fear. He's here for the weekend.

"I'm going out for a swim. You coming?"

"In a bit. I need to catch my breath and call the doctor back first."

He crosses the room to the window behind me. "Have you eaten? I could go to town and pick up some meat. Light up the barbeque, get a few beers?"

Be nice. He's trying.

"Sure, why not? I need to call—"

"It's over thirty-five in the south of England today, can you imagine—"

"Paddy, please. I need to finish here. Why don't you ask Scarlett if she'd like to go with you to the lake? I'll be finished here when you come back."

"I'll do that, so, yeah. She downstairs?"

I nod.

He leaves, shouting back, "Coffee?"

"Too late."

"Beer, wine, vodka?"

"Too early." I restart the Zoom call, and the now poker-faced doctor joins the meeting. "Dr Goldberg, I've booked the hotel. I'll send on the itinerary—"

At the top of his voice, Paddy calls Scarlett.

"Everything is in order for next week. I think €40 per ticket will cover..."

Bang.

"You requested that someone meet you at the airport. I would be honoured to do that. I'd love to show you around."

Crash.

I stand to close the office door, when Paddy almost runs straight into me, his face beetroot.

"Where did you say Scarlett is?"

"Downstairs. In the kitchen." I smile through gritted teeth. The doctor tuts on-screen.

"She's not downstairs."

"Did you try her room?"

"Just did. She's not there."

"Can you excuse me for one moment, please?" I ask the doctor, muting the mic and turning off the camera. "Paddy! Can this not wait?"

He rubs his jawline. "She's not in the garden either."

"Front or back?"

"Front AND back. This isn't good. Can you come, please? Finish your chat another time."

"Are you still there? Oh, for Pete's sake," the doctor snaps.

I unmute. "Something's come up."

"Fine. I'm going." The doctor's Zoom face blanks out.

I'm practically crying with frustration. "Paddy, you knew that was important—"

"Scarlett's not here." Paddy paces the study, hands on hips. "If that's not important, I don't know what is."

"Of course she's here. Stop panicking," I tell him. "She's always doing this, hiding out. She's a bloody master of disguise." I go into Scarlett's bedroom. Pink bedclothes, pink curtains and pink butterflied wallpaper covered in her sketches and paintings. "Come out, come out, wherever you are. I give up, you win." I look under her single bed and in cupboards, behind her curtains and even in her toy box. Nothing.

Paddy stands behind me. "See? She's not here."

He follows me downstairs through the living room and into the kitchen, where white voile curtains flutter against the open French doors. The house is quiet except for the distant summer sounds from the lake and our voices. I call again, this time louder. "*Scarlett, come out, come out wherever you are.*"

"I'll check the back garden again. Check the front," Paddy says.

I dash to the front of the house and open the hall door to a wall of heat. My starched shirt is suffocating under the beating sun. The front landscaped lawn with its neatly trimmed hedges, bushes, my red Astra and Paddy's black Merc has morphed into a maze. I search every inch. She must be here; she has to be. I check the doors of our cars to find them locked, then spreadeagle on the gravel below them, but there is nothing and nobody under either car.

The noise of the tractor stops. I lean over the small pebble-dashed wall at the end of the driveway, shading my eyes with my hand, and scan the length of our road, a narrow boreen with grass growing down the middle. The tractor is far in the distance, and there is no way into that field.

Paddy comes from around the side of the house and stands in the middle of the road with his hands on his head. "Still no reason to panic?"

"She wouldn't go off on her own; she must be inside." I return to the kitchen, where Scarlett's brushes sit in a jar of cloudy water surrounded by new paintings on the grey kitchen table. I run the ball of my left index finger over one of them. A ginger cat. Dry to the touch.

The voile curtain lifts as a gentle breeze blows through the open back doors. "They were open when I got home," Paddy says.

"The playhouse," we chorus together.

Scarlett can hide forever, but gets bored and sneaks back to her playhouse when nobody is watching and entertains herself there. She has the patience of a stealth spy once she's back in her little haven.

Together, we hurry to the bottom of our long, sloped

lawn. I open the door of her wooden playhouse, praying to find her playing with dolls or her chalkboard or something, but to no avail.

"I'll check the shed," Paddy says, but stops as he passes the back gate. The seven-foot-tall metal gate that leads to the lake shore.

The previous owners installed it to stop trouble coming from the lake, which was strange because we never had a moment's trouble since we moved in. I follow Paddy, saying a silent prayer. *Please, God, let it be—*

"It's locked," he confirms.

Thank God.

"Does she know where the key is?" he asks.

"Yes, but she wouldn't go out without telling me. She knows she's not allowed near the lake without one of us, and she's never done it before. I'll make sure the key is still inside on the hook."

"Can you grab the key for the shed while you're there?"

I'm halfway up the garden when Paddy calls after me, "What time did you last see Scarlett?"

I turn. "Good question. Before I started my call at six. No, I was upstairs preparing first, so more like half past five."

His mouth falls open. "Half past five? Karen, that's over an hour ago. It's almost seven!" He holds his phone out to show me the time: 6:45pm.

No, that can't be right. I put my hand into my shorts pocket, then remember that I gave Scarlett my phone earlier to play with. "Scarlett had my phone. Ring it."

Paddy calls my number, and my ringtone plays from inside the house. We follow the upbeat pop tune to the kitchen table to find a painting vibrating on the kitchen table. I lift it, dreading what I know I will find. My phone.

"That's it," Paddy says. "I'm calling the police."

2

I go from room to room with barely suppressed hysteria, calling out, "Scarlett, come on now. Game's over. You're scaring us."

Paddy hands his phone to me. "It's calling Mullingar Garda Station. They'll want to talk to you because you're the mother." I try to object, not trusting myself to make any sense or form words, but the dial tone stops, and the call is answered.

"Mullingar Garda Station. Garda Jack Flynn speaking."

I step out into the back garden, where Scarlett's swing set sits still on the grass, her present when we moved from the apartment to here.

"Hello. Garda Flynn here. How can I help you?"

"Um." I rub the sweat from my eyes. "My daughter. We can't find her." I won't say the *m* word. That will make it real. I won't do that.

"Can I take your name and number?" he asks.

"Scarlett, come on, baby. Game's over now. I give up. You win. Come on." Paddy opens the large metal shed left by the previous owners at the bottom of the garden and drags our new lawnmower out. I hate that shed, but he says we should keep it because the lake is so close, and a wooden shed will rot in the elements.

"Ma'am?" the Garda asks.

"Oh, um, sorry. It's Karen O'Hara, Lough Owel Lodge, Mullingar."

"Hello, Karen. You say you can't find your daughter. Are you at home?"

Paddy wheels a rusty barbeque, which squeaks and clangs its way down the small concrete path. The previous owners left the shed full of old rubbish, which we will clean out as soon as we get a chance, although they left the play-house, which Scarlett loved from day one. She is probably back there now.

"Yes, we're at home," I say, already on my way to check again.

"What age is she?"

"Eight. Scarlett is eight years old."

"Scarlett, eight years old. When did you see her last?"

"About half past five this afternoon. She was downstairs. I had an online meeting in the office upstairs." The playhouse door is open from earlier, but it's still empty. A wave of nausea washes over me, and I crumple onto the white sun lounger. We bought three plastic loungers from the local hardware centre when we moved in. I wanted to get a classic matching garden set, but Scarlett insisted on this exact chair, and that we all choose a different colour. I chose white, Paddy chose blue and Scarlett pink, of course.

"I'm going to get a car around to you, because she's so young and she's been missing over an hour."

I leap to my feet. "No, that's not right, Garda. Not that long. Half five is when I last saw her—" But even as I say the words, reality hits. It could be that long.

"I mean since you saw her," he clarifies. "Are you still at home now, Karen?"

Paddy gestures for to me to hurry up and end the call. He has covered the lawn with most of the shed's contents.

"Yes, we're home. Can you please come?"

"As quick as we can. I'll just need to get a quick description first."

"Her name is Scarlett O'Hara. She's eight years old with dark brown curly hair, blue eyes and freckles. She's wearing a T-shirt and shorts, is of medium build and about four feet tall. And deaf."

There is a pause. "She's deaf? Okay, well, um... the officers coming out won't have sign language. There's a number for an interpreter I can call..."

"She doesn't need an interpreter. Sure, she can use sign language, but she has cochlear implants."

"Okay. Tell me, when was it you noticed her gone?"

"It was my husband who noticed. He came home about half past six, so" – I hold the phone out to read the time from the screen – "twenty minutes ago." Time is moving too quickly.

"And where is your husband now?"

"He's here." I hold the phone out to Paddy, who drops the wheelbarrow and comes towards me. "I'll put him on."

"No need right now. Have you called anyone? Does she have a phone, buddies, a pet?"

"We're only here a few months. She hasn't started her new school yet and no pets."

"And a phone?"

"No, no phone."

"Right. Has she gone off herself before?"

"No. She's a good kid."

"What I'm going to do is send a car around to you. They'll get more details when they arrive. I'm also going to ring the lifeguards to have a look along the lake shore in case she wandered out there."

My stomach lurches. "The back gate was locked, and it's the only way out there. She can't be on the lake."

"Have you been out around the lake?" he asks, and a million possibilities flood my brain, all ending with a body. But that's ridiculous because she can't—

"We'll go out to the lake now," Paddy says into the phone.

"Do that," the Garda says, "keep this phone switched on, and we'll call when we arrive. Can I ask you to have a recent photograph ready for us?"

"You can take any from my Facebook page: Scarlett Hears," I say. Paddy shakes his head at me.

"Can I ask you to do that for us? It will save time, and if there is anything else you can think of in the meantime that we should know, please call back."

"She can hear and speak with her implants but won't hear you from a distance. If her implants are off, she won't hear anything or anybody. What if she's lying injured somewhere or if someone has her and took her implants off and... she hates the silence and..." I can't continue.

"Karen, let's work on getting her back. A car is on its way, and we'll cover all bases. If she comes home in the meantime, please give me a ring back. Ask for Garda Jack Flynn."

"Please hurry, Garda Flynn." I sob.

"Fifteen minutes. They'll be with you in fifteen minutes."

"Thank you." I end the call and follow Paddy through the now-open metal gate onto the shore of Lough Owel. The stony shoreline runs about two hundred metres and is held in by forestry to the east and west and the vast Lough Owel to the front, which is as smooth as a sheet of glass today. Ours is the only house that backs onto the shore at this point of the lake. I usually love being out here. It's a favourite spot for freshwater swimmers and a social destination for the whole of Mullingar on summer days. From the moment Paddy found this old farmhouse, I fell in love with it and the area. It reminded me of swimming and exploring in Galway as a child. When I could disappear all day and nobody cared. Different times.

About fifty meters to the right of us, a group of half-naked young teens with buff physiques play-act, pushing each other off the long diving board and into the deep rocky water. Rap music blares expletives as sun-kissed families move in every direction with inflatable rings and miniature dogs on leads. The car park on the hill is always full on a hot day like today. It's all so normal, so typical of a summer's day here in the midlands, and so bloody wrong.

We turn right and begin our search of the strand, passing a whistling man barbecuing sausages and burgers surrounded by excited children. There is no sign of her.

"Excuse me, have you seen a little girl, eight years old, brown hair, pink T-shirt about yay high?" I ask, and he shakes his head.

"Check past the diving board. There were some little ones paddling down there earlier."

The lake stretches to fifty different shades of green on the faraway shore. Low and clear, it should be a dream vista, but today all I can see is a vast deathtrap. Past the diving board, five or six little girls run into the water. Even though it's a hot day, the lake is always cold, and I draw breath as they hit the water, shrieking, before collapsing in giggles. She's not there, and I want to scream at them, at everyone, to stop having fun and help us.

Paddy sloshes through the water at the shore in his work trousers and blue shirt, his eyes red and his face puffy. He turns to me. "Where is my Scarlett O'Hara?" and with that, I'm back in the hospital and the moment he first called her that name. *It was touch-and-go. We almost lost her.*

A couple carrying a red kayak enter the water beside us and paddle away from the shore. Paddy wipes his eyes and splashes through the resistant water, his phone in his outstretched hand, but they're too fast, and he's too late. A gang of gothic-looking teenagers lie in the grass back from the water. Paddy approaches them, and they scramble to hide whatever they're smoking, but when he shows them his phone, they shake their heads to a chorus of *No, mans*.

To my left, a young couple kiss on a red tartan blanket on the grass bank, engrossed in each other. I'm about to ask them when the ringtone from Paddy's phone pierces the air. He answers, moving away from the teenagers. "Uh-huh... sure. We'll be right there."

He beckons me. "The Gardai. They're here."

3

I open the front door to two guards in navy uniforms, a
tall, grey-haired, middle-aged man and a shorter,
younger, dark-haired woman who stands back and
surveys our house from the driveway.

"Garda Cormac McCarthy," he says, "and this is my
colleague Garda Helen Ryan. You called about your daughter,
Scarlett?"

"Yes. Thank you for coming." My voice tapers off as I fight
to hold back the tears.

"Take your time. Karen, is it?"

"Yes, it is." Paddy answers from the hallway behind me
and places his hand on the small of my back. "I'm Paddy,
Scarlett's dad." He offers his hand, and Garda McCarthy
shakes it.

"Garda Helen Ryan." She steps forward and shakes
Paddy's hand. She has piercing brown eyes, and her hair is
cut short. "Any luck since you called?"

"No, nothing yet. We were on the lake when you called;
she isn't there."

"Is it alright if we come in?"

"Of course, please." I stand aside, and Paddy leads the Gardai in out of the sun. As she passes me, Garda Ryan pulls at her collar.

"Can I get you a glass of water?"

"I'm fine, but appreciate the offer. It's so hot out there."

I follow them into the living room and offer them a seat. They sit in the pinstriped upholstered armchairs, and I take my place beside Paddy on the white leather couch in the bay window, charging my phone beside me.

Garda McCarthy flips open his notebook. "I'm going to ask you a few questions, folks, so we can get moving. You've had a good look inside and outside the house?"

"Everywhere," Paddy answers, rubbing his hands on his trousers.

"And she hasn't got a phone?"

"Too young."

"I let her use my phone for YouTube and that," I explain. "She had it today, but it was still in the kitchen after we noticed she was g... not there."

"Have you called around the neighbours?"

"We don't have neighbours," I say. "The closest people to us are the Devlins, but they're a good kilometre away. There was a tractor working across the way today, but there is no way into that field from here. We're quite isolated except for the lake at the back."

"It's one of the reasons we chose this place," Paddy says. "We moved from the city."

"Do you have CCTV yourselves?"

I glance at Paddy. I wanted to get CCTV and high elec-tronic gates installed out front before we moved in, but he resisted, claiming I was overreacting, and once we moved, we would be safe in such a remote place. The house is right down the end of a long lane, with high fences at the back, and he felt we would ruin the vista. It was hard to get Paddy to part with money at the best of times, but there was no chance when he wasn't on board with an idea, so I dropped it, on condition that at the first sign of trouble, we would revisit the decision.

There was no trouble, and I adored it here from day one. Waking up to the scent of wild herbs, pottering barefoot in a kitchen overlooking the lake, I left the noise, and stress, of the overcrowded city behind. I'm mad now I didn't push harder for CCTV, but it's not the time for a blame game. God knows, I could play that game.

"No CCTV," I say. "This road is off the beaten track. Unless someone is lost, delivering or visiting, they have no business coming down this way."

Garda McCarthy turns his page. "We'll go up the lane and call in to your neighbours, Eileen and Christy."

"Oh, you know the Devlins?" I ask.

He catches his colleague's eye. "We know the Devlins."

"Christy is our gardener," I say, "but the Devlins are right up the top of the lane. She wouldn't go up that far. Not without telling me. Not by herself."

"Has there been anyone else around? Workers, tradespeople? Delivery drivers? Anyone who could have seen her?"

"No. Not this week. Sometimes we get food delivered but not this week. We got a lot of work done on the house, but they finished over a month ago."

"Is there anywhere else she could have gone except up the lane?"

"Two options from here," I say, "up the lane or through the back gate onto the lake shore, but the back gate was locked."

"With a key?"

"Yes, a key, and it was still in the kitchen on its hook. There's only one."

Garda Ryan takes a notebook from her shirt pocket.

"Folks, I'm going to ask a few more questions. I know this is hard, but the more information we have, the better. Karen, the last time you saw Scarlett was around 5:30pm, correct?"

"Yes, but we didn't realise she was gone until Paddy came home, around half past six. She could have been here anytime up until then."

"Scarlett O'Hara, eight years old, dark brown curly hair, blue eyes and freckles, medium build and four feet in height. Shorts, T-shirt, and deaf with cochlear implants."

I swallow a lump in my throat, and Paddy squeezes my hand.

"My colleague asked you to have a picture ready for us?"

"Yes, I have one from yesterday here."

"Can you send it to my WhatsApp?" She gives me her number, and I send her a picture of Scarlett on our trip to the zoo.

She checks her phone. "Got it. She's a little beauty."

Her kindness releases a valve, and my tears stream, hot and heavy.

"Now, this might seem insensitive, but I have to ask. Were there any arguments or tensions this week?"

"I don't think so," Paddy says, offering me a tissue from the box on the coffee table.

She leans forward, resting her notebook. "Take a moment, Karen. In your own time."

I dab my eyes. "No arguments."

"What exactly was Scarlett wearing when you saw her last?"

Saw her last.

"Pink – her favourite colour. Yeah, a baby-pink T-shirt with an ice-cream cone on the front, light-blue denim shorts, and pink diamanté shoes. She might have had white socks on too."

"And her hair? How was she wearing that?"

"In a ponytail. She could have taken it down. She does that sometimes, but I prefer her to have it up so I can see her lights. They tell me when her batteries need charging. Oh God, her batteries. What time is it?"

She checks her watch. "Seven fifteen, I'm going as fast—"

"Her batteries. They'll die in a few hours. Then she'll be in complete silence. She's terrified of the dark and the quiet." I put my head between my knees to stop myself from vomiting or passing out, or both.

"Karen, look at me," Garda Ryan demands. "Look at me!"

I force myself to make eye contact with her.

"We will do everything we can to find Scarlett, I promise you that. If, and I'm not saying they will, but if the batteries die, what can she hear without her implants?"

"Nothing. They're her ears."

Garda McCarthy comes in. "At the risk of sounding ignorant, do you mind explaining what cochlear implants are?"

I twirl the tissue around my fingers. "Electronic devices that bypass the damaged part of the ear." I catch myself and consider the simplest and quickest way to explain. "Most of it is inside her head, but outside, it is like a hearing aid with discs on her head."

"Are they in the picture you sent me?" Garda Ryan asks, tapping her phone screen.

Paddy paces. "This is taking too long. We need to find her."

"Yes, they're in the picture," I reply. "She wears them every waking moment. The discs are brown, they blend with her hair, so you mightn't be able to see them."

"Can we get out and find her?" Paddy exclaims. "It's getting late, and we've answered all your questions."

"Mr O'Hara, we all want to get your daughter home," Garda Ryan says.

He bites his lip.

"Go on. Please," I say. "The sooner we answer, the sooner we can get out there."

"Is Scarlett on TikTok or any of those apps?"

"God no. So dangerous. You don't know who you are talking to," I say, and Paddy clicks his tongue.

"One last thing." She closes her notebook. "Would she go with someone unfamiliar to her?"

We chorus together, "No."

She stands. "That's it for the moment. We'll get a search going once we take a quick look around the house."

"Of course." Paddy stands.

"Sorry, one more thing?" Garda McCarthy says. "Is there GPS on the implants, by any chance?"

"Yes!" Paddy clicks his fingers. "How did we not think of it? Karen, the app! The app will show us where she is." He's scrolling through his phone before I can reply.

"Paddy, I—" He's not listening. Garda Ryan watches me.

"Paddy, please, listen—"

He holds his index finger up for me to wait, and I don't know whether to scream or cry.

"I'm in the app now," Paddy says.

Garda Ryan raises an eyebrow at me.

"It connects our phones to Scarlett's implants," I explain.

"The implants have GPS, then?" Garda McCarthy asks.

"Bluetooth, not GPS," I say. "The implants must be within twenty metres or so of the phone to connect."

Paddy stops tapping, and his mouth falls open.

"What is it?" Garda Ryan asks.

"She's here, in the house." Paddy shows us a red dot throbbing on a wireframe map on his phone. Over our house. "Scarlett's here."

"Paddy, the app shows the last time *your phone* was in contact with her implants when they were on."

"But it shows her here."

"What date?"

He furrows his brow and whispers, "Thursday."

"When you left this morning, Scarlett was asleep. Her implants were on their charging dock. They weren't switched on."

I turn to the Gardai, and they look as puzzled as Paddy.

"Consider wireless headphones," I say. "To connect to the phone, they need to be switched on and paired, right? It's the same principle with her cochlear implants."

Paddy clicks his fingers again. "Karen, check your phone. You were here all day; we'll be able to see the last time she was here."

I lower my gaze. "They won't show on mine."

"They will. You were here. She had her implants on today. You said she did. Check your phone."

My heart is racing. "I hadn't got my Bluetooth switched on."

"There'll be a record of some sort. Try."

I unplug my phone and key in my PIN code. Paddy swipes it out of my hand. I try to grab it back, but he's too fast.

"The app, the cochlear app. Karen, where do you have the app?"

"Will you listen to me? I deleted it."

Paddy lifts his head, his voice low and slow. "You did what?"

I hold back the tears. "I deleted the app."

He pinches the bridge of his nose with the thumb and index finger of his left hand. "Why would you do that?"

"To download a hotel booking app for Dr Goldberg."

I wouldn't expect him to understand with his latest iPhone and its space for a million apps. All three of them are staring at me.

Paddy holds his head in his hands. "I don't believe this."

"My phone is old. I have very little storage."

"Paddy," Garda Ryan says, her voice calm, "when did you last see Scarlett?"

"This morning. In her room. She was fast asleep, so I didn't wake her."

"We'll take that look around, okay?" Together with Garda McCarthy, she examines the entire house, inside and out.

When they finish, Garda Ryan sticks her head into the living room. "We're done for the moment. We were thinking, if all our colleagues download the app, we might find her easier."

"The app must be logged in to and paired physically with the implants to work. Only myself and Paddy are paired with Scarlett's implants."

"Can you stay here?" she asks when I show them to the door.

"I can't stay here, doing nothing. My daughter is missing." I recoil as the word leaves my mouth. *I used the word missing.* I've crossed an invisible line.

"You need to be here in case she comes back, but there's plenty you can do. Call around – friends, family, and if you think of anything that could help us, please call. I'll impart all this information to our colleagues, and a liaison officer will be appointed to you."

I think of the valuable time we'd waste going through all these questions again. "Could you be our liaison officer?"

Garda Ryan shrugs. "I can if that's what you want."

"Yes," I say. "We would like that."

I close the front door as the Gardai drive out the front gate. Leaning against it, I take a deep breath.

"I'm going up the lane." Paddy won't look at me. "Will you download the implant app again and switch on your Bluetooth?"

"Of course I will, Paddy." He still won't make eye contact. "Hey, don't do that. This is not my fault."

He leans across me to open the door.

"It was only an hour, Paddy. An hour. For God's sake."

He exhales and steps outside.

"I'll ring my mother and Jess." I follow him. "Will you ring your crew – work and that?"

"Fat lot of good ringing your mother will do and her in Portugal."

"It's better she hears it from me first. I'll do a Facebook Live too. Wait, the microphone." I dash to fetch the FM transmitter from its charging dock in the white cabinet in the living room. Taking it outside, I hang it around Paddy's neck. "She'll hear you now like you're beside her."

"I think I know how this works, Karen." He fixes the lanyard around his shirt collar with more than a hint of contempt and unlocks his Merc. He should know how it works, but I'm not sure he did until this minute. He may be a technical partner, but he has little to no interest in Scarlett's implants or the many accessories that help her in life. *A busman's holiday*, he calls it when I try to involve him, saying he lives technology twenty-four seven, but I think it is more than that. His head-in-the-sand approach to Scarlett's equipment is classic denial: that if he doesn't acknowledge it, she can't be deaf, and if she isn't deaf, then it can't be his fault.

But it is his fault. All of it.

4

Eight years ago

I try to open my eyes, but the brightness hurts, so I lift my right hand to provide shade when a pain shoots up my arm. There's something in my hand, a needle I think, yes, a needle with a tube leading from it. I follow the tube with the fingers of my left hand and fight to makes sense of it, but a wave of exhaustion and nausea washes over me. I'll close my eyes for a minute.

I wake again. Where am I? I can't think; a grey fuzz is throbbing in my head. My legs are as heavy as the air, the stench of bleach and blood overpowering. A gentle breeze passes over me as a woman laughs in the distance. Footsteps pass forwards and backwards close by. This is lovely.

I don't know if I drifted off, but someone is holding my wrist. I force my eyes open to see a dark-haired nurse with a chart.

"Good morning." She smiles at me, then continues writing.

I lift my head to look around the tiny room. There's a grey

plastic chair to my left, and a TV hangs at the foot of my bed, over a table with a vase of yellow roses and a Get Well Soon card. An open door in the corner reveals a white toilet and a red cord. The top window is open, a breeze flowing through the room, rattling the door. Outside people walk by, chatting.

"Where am I?"

She hangs the chart at the foot of my bed and sits on the plastic chair. "St Mary's hospital, love. I'm Anne, one of the nurses who's been looking after you. You've been through the mill, but you're in good hands."

I follow her eyes as they move to a pink waffle blanket over my bed, covering the flatness where my bump should be.

Boom! It floods back. In my car after the pregnancy scan. The phone. The lorry. *Smash.*

I jolt up, my head exploding with pain, and I cry out, "Where's my bump?"

Anne rubs my hand, her face pained, and I know. I know. "One moment, love. I'll get your husband; he's just gone down for a cuppa."

She leaves the room, and I lift the blanket, peering underneath to find I am wearing a mint green and white hospital gown, and there is a catheter leading to the clear bag of yellow liquid at the side of my bed. I lift the gown to see my abdomen, to find it bandaged and my stomach dimpled like a deflated balloon.

Anne returns with a dishevelled Paddy in tow wearing jeans and a navy hoodie, his unshaven face grey. He rushes to me, throwing his arms around me, and bursts into tears.

"Oh, thank God. You're awake. I was so worried." He pulls back. "How are you? Are you in pain?"

I shake my heavy head. "What happened?"

He sits on the side of my bed and takes my hand with the catheter in his. "We were in a car accident, and you were badly injured. They were blessed to get you out, but you were bleeding so heavily. You had an emergency C-section. At twenty-six weeks, Hope's lungs were too weak, but she fought, Karen. She fought like a little warrior for three whole days." Great big tears stream down his face.

"They did everything they could, Karen. Honestly, they did, but she was too small and too ill. She couldn't stay here with us." He swallows. "She passed away three weeks ago, peacefully and in no pain."

"I've been asleep for over three weeks?" A sickening emotion like I have never experienced before pierces my drugged haze. Paddy rocks me as I wail, zoning in and out. My poor baby. My poor Hope.

Paddy pushes back my hair and forces a smile through his tears. "But Scarlett made it. She contracted sepsis and was critical, but she pulled through."

"Who's Scarlett?"

His eyes glisten. "Our daughter. The most beautiful baby in the world. She's upstairs in the ICU." He turns to the nurse. "Anne, can I take Karen to see Scarlett?"

"We can arrange that once she's strong enough, but I think she should rest for the moment."

The next day, Paddy and Anne accompany me as a hospital porter wheels me to the neonatal ward. He puts on the wheelchair brakes beside an incubator with the name Scarlett O'Hara. "I'll come back in a bit," he says.

Scarlett O'Hara. That's not right. Elenora Sullivan O'Hara. We agreed.

In the incubator lies a baby in the tiniest nappy I have ever seen, swamped in a sea of wires and surrounded by beeping monitors.

"Hello, my little Scarlett O'Hara." Paddy's face brims with love. "Mammy's here. Say hello, Mammy."

"Hello, um, Scarlett?" I wish I could think straight, but this doesn't rest easy with me.

Paddy frowns. "You don't mind that I changed her name, do you?"

I don't think I do. Hope was my choice, and Elenora was his. It's a tradition that the first granddaughter in Paddy's family takes the name Elenora, going back generations. His own mother's name was that, and she insisted it continue through to our first daughter, Paddy being her first and only child.

I rub my head. "What about your mother?"

"Isn't she amazing?" He beams, ignoring my question and keeping his eyes on the baby. "It was touch-and-go. We almost lost her too."

"Why did you change her name?"

"Elenora was too big a name for such a little one, and her skin, Karen, you should have seen it, it was so red and transparent. I began calling her Scarlett O'Hara, as in Vivienne Leigh in *Gone with the Wind*, but then it suited her. With Scarlett, the Sullivan didn't make sense anymore."

The baby moves her hand and clenches a tiny fist. "All that matters is she's going to be okay. She's perfect."

He bites his lip. "There were complications from the gentamicin, the drug that saved her life, but look at her, Karen. She's spectacular."

"What complications?"

"She has grown so strong."

"What complications?" I repeat.

He rubs his jaw.

"Paddy!"

He raises his head, his eyes red yet again. "She failed her newborn hearing screening."

My hand flies to my mouth. "She's deaf?"

He steps away from me. "They don't know. Hearing loss is

a known complication from the drug, but it could be fluid. They'll run the tests again before we leave. We'll manage though, we will."

I struggle to take in the news while Paddy is doe-eyed, taking pictures of the baby in the incubator like he is father of the year. Her bare chest rises and falls, her head in a tiny hat. She is so vulnerable, but she's here, and the love that fills me is like nothing I have ever experienced.

Unwelcome thoughts surface. She'll never meet her sister, and now, she could be deaf. Paddy's phone rings, and I'm back in the car before the crash again. I told him not to answer it, but he wouldn't listen. The car hurtling across the road, the lorry coming at full speed, the phone in mid-air, is followed by a throbbing head and a black void.

He wouldn't listen, and now one of his daughters is dead, and his other might be deaf. Never knowing her sister, hearing birdsong or music, talking or saying the word "Mama."

He did this.

5

Missing 3 hours

With Paddy gone to look for Scarlett, I'm alone in the empty house. When we first moved in, it was in terrible shape, but a new kitchen, floors and cupboards along with painters and decorators transformed it into a wonderful place to be. I love the peace here normally, but it's too quiet; I have to do something. Contact anyone I can think of, the Garda said. I call Jess, my best friend and the soundest person I know, but her phone goes to voicemail.

"Hi, it's Jess. Leave a message."

"Hi, Jess. It's Karen. Call me as soon as you get this. It's urgent."

I call my mother, and her phone goes to voicemail too. I leave her the same message. There's nobody else I can think of who can help except for the Devlins, and I don't have a number for them.

If I did a live video, I could kill two birds with the one stone – reach as many people as possible and stop myself from losing my mind. I fill a glass of tap water and fetch my laptop, clearing a space on the kitchen table. The adjacent wall is covered in Scarlett's artwork. I turn my back to it; I can't handle seeing her pictures right now. I ring my mother again, but it goes to voicemail.

I save two JPEG pictures to the desktop – a recent one of Scarlett and a stock image of a cochlear implant. I say a silent prayer and go live.

Three – two – one. Facebook Live.

"Hi, guys, it's Karen. We need your help. Since half past five this evening, my daughter, Scarlett, is—" My breath catches, but I have to push through. "She is... we can't find her anywhere."

I take a sip of water to steady myself. My hand trembles as I share the picture of Scarlett eating an ice-cream cone, and I weaken at her little freckled face. "If anyone has seen her, please let us know. Share this picture far and wide. Keep an eye out for her. If you see her, that would be... I don't know... the Gardai are... please help. Share this post or do what you can. I don't know—" I stifle a sob.

The eye icon in the corner of my screen shows twelve people watching. The comments start.

Jane Newman: Lovely day here in Cork.

Angela Wright: Hi.

Jo Kennedy: Long time no hear.

The time delay between posting and seeing the comments is cruel. I wait for them to catch up on the live stream.

Jane Newman: OMG Sharing now.

Angela Wright: Sharing in Dublin. What height is she?

Pete Johnson: Can you give us a full description?

"A description, yes. She's eight years old, four feet in height, normal build, with long curly brown hair. She's wearing a pink T-shirt with an ice-cream cone on the front, blue denim shorts with pink shoes. She's deaf with cochlear implants like these."

I share the picture of the implants. Forty-eight people have tuned in.

Mama love: Sharing. Please God, bring the little angel home safe.

Keira Malone: Where do you live?

"Our house is a little outside Mullingar on the shore of Lough Owel. If you live nearby, can you check around your house and any sheds, outhouses or abandoned buildings? She could have fallen and banged her head. If she knocked her implants off, she won't hear you calling, so have a really good look. If she's locked in somewhere or lying in a..." My voice croaks. I can't continue.

Sixty-three watching.

Fiona Sheridan: Can't come but sharing in Offaly.

New man: Only a few hours ago, hardly a missing child, I've taken longer craps.

Keira Malone: @New Man The first 24 hours are crucial. That's why this is urgent, dumbass.

I take another sip of water. "Her implants are powered by specialised batteries and can't have much battery power left. I charged them last night, but Scarlett has been up since 8am, and she's had her implants on since then. She gets a day and a half out of them max and is petrified of the silence, which means we have to find her."

Dodge Geeza: How many likes will you get for this, Karen? #MediaWhore

Angela Wright: @Dodge Geeza Shut your mouth. This is awful.

Mum of two: I only get 8 hours out of my batteries.

Shelley Graham: I get 20 out of mine, get that checked.

Hannah Mahoney: Shared in Lucan, Dublin.

My phone rings with a number I don't recognise. I reject the call.

Ivy Drumm: Why are you on Facebook instead of searching for your kid?

"Please contact me anytime or call the police if you think of anything, no matter how small."

The doorbell rings. I put my number in the chat and share the picture of Scarlett on-screen again, then scan through the comments, which are flying in and supportive, but one jumps out.

You need a license for a dog, yet bitches like you get to have kids. I thought you were cancelled.

I slam my laptop shut before I can read any more. I can't stay here; they're right – what am I doing? Scarlett is missing. The doorbell rings again, this time for longer. I open the door to find Garda Ryan standing there, and burst into tears.

———

I LEAN on the white island counter in the kitchen, shading my eyes from the sinking evening sun, and explain to Garda Ryan what happened online.

"Call me Helen." She hands me a cup of tea. "I won't pretend to understand the whole social media world, but there are a lot of sick people out there – very brave behind their keyboards."

"They're not wrong though; I am a terrible mother."

"Why do you say that?"

I take a sip. "I've been distracted. Killing myself to cater for a woman I don't even know, meanwhile neglecting my child. In the last two weeks, we've done no speech or occupational therapy or homework, and I can't remember the last time we read a book together. Organising a conference to help other parents, and yes, for the kudos, has drained every bit of my time and energy."

She leans on the counter towards me. "You have to earn a living."

"Paddy says it's a hobby not a job. I don't make any money. I used to run a blog, well, I used to do a lot of stuff – writing articles, vlogging, helping people, especially mothers dealing with diagnoses of hearing loss and postpartum depression. It kept me sane, as Paddy's working hours are mental. Things slowed down there for me in the last year, and this conference is a huge opportunity to prove myself, but it doesn't pay. So yeah, it's a hobby, not a job."

"That's impressive."

"Hmmm. Is it? I wanted to help people who found themselves in the same situation as us. When Scarlett was diagnosed as deaf, I found it very tough. She was the first deaf or hard-of-hearing person in both Paddy's and my family. It was a whole new world and a lot to take in. Then all the information, the appointments, the cochlear implant journey and so many opinions. It was exhausting and, if I'm honest, dreadfully lonely. Paddy worked harder than ever to support us and pay for the road ahead; my mother was abroad, and his mother wasn't – still isn't – talking to us. My colleagues continued to work the long hours I once did, and it felt like life moved on without me."

"That must have been hard."

"Well, what doesn't kill you makes you stronger, right? I vowed to remember how that felt and to do what I could for those coming after. I loved the blogging and all that comes with it. I'm open, Paddy says way too open."

"Did you get any media training?"

"No. My background is in IT – computers, but I have no social media training. Sometimes late at night when I can't sleep, intrusive thoughts that I spend time with strangers to avoid spending time with my own family seep in."

Helen nods towards Scarlett's paintings on the far wall. "Who did those?"

The wall is covered in brightly painted pictures of animals and stick people.

"Scarlett."

"They're good... as kids' art goes."

"Have you got children yourself?"

"Five of them, and even though I love the little rascals, I run out that door every morning. I don't think that makes me a bad mother. If anything, it makes me better; keeps me sane. Like this hobby, passion, whatever it is for you."

She takes my empty cup to our white square sink. "Now,

about Scarlett. We have raised an Amber Alert, and an incident room has been set up in the station, headed up by DI McGovern. The Community Policing Bike Unit has been dispatched, and all available cars and personnel are out, going door to door and combing the shore. CCTV is being seized, and outhouses and sheds are also being checked. If nothing shows, we'll call the coastguard, the helicopter unit and the dogs. Trust me, we will leave no stone unturned, and let's say no more social media without running it through us first."

A thought pops into my head. "What if someone has her? A paedophile? A murderer?"

She doesn't flinch. "Do you know of anyone who would want to take her?"

"No." I don't.

"Well, let's not go there."

My phone rings. A number I don't recognise, but it could be information.

"Hello, Karen speaking."

"Show us your tits," a man says to a background of raucous laughter. Helen whips the phone from me. "Garda Ryan speaking. Who is this?"

The line goes dead, and she hands back my phone. "I will never understand the mentality of some people."

The front door opens, and Paddy dashes in. "The Devlins said we can look at their CCTV."

"I'll take you," Helen says. "Let me radio a colleague to come here while we're gone." Within minutes another Garda arrives, and Helen drives us up the dirt lane to the Devlins' house. It's an original thatched cottage on the T-junction as the road slopes downwards to our house. A traditional dwelling with a yard that comes from one road, scoops around the back of their house and leads onto the other. Old machinery and bits of tractors litter the dirt yard, and hens scarper as we drive in. A monstrous Alsatian runs to the car, snarling and barking. Mrs Devlin runs from the back door, grabs the dog by the collar and waits for us while the dog watches with her ears pricked.

"She wouldn't hurt a fly, but she's a great guard dog. It's her job, isn't that right, Maxi?" The dog falls onto her back and allows Mrs Devlin to rub her belly.

"Eileen," Helen greets the old woman.

"Helen," Mrs Devlin greets the Garda. The dog stands and saunters into the shade of the house, where she collapses and licks her paws. We follow the grey-haired heavyset old lady through her green wooden back door, her tiny kitchen and into a whitewashed living room. Paddy stoops to avoid the low wooden beams and takes a seat at the wooden table in the living room. The smell of cats is pungent, no doubt amplified by the turf fire blazing up the chimney.

An open laptop sits on the table. "Take a seat," Mrs Devlin says, staying standing herself. "Freddie, our son, got the laptop for us when he was home from Australia. I've tea in the pot. Can I get you a cup?"

We decline the tea. I'd imagine, like me, none of us want to linger in this furnace longer than is necessary, under the glare of the up-lit statue of the Virgin Mary on the opposite wall. There is a loud bang from upstairs.

"There's Christy now," Mrs Devlin says. The low ceiling creaks, and her husband appears at the top of the stairs in a string vest and brown trousers, rubbing his groggy face.

"Woman, don't tell me you've a fire on today, and it the hottest day of the year?"

He stops on the bottom step when he sees us. "What's going on?"

He's different from the balding smiley man in overalls who comes to do our garden every week. Older. Sterner.

"The little one is missing, so we're checking the CCTV,"

Mrs Devlin says, and he holds his hand out for her to wait. He goes to the sideboard and takes two white hearing aids from a metal box, popping them into his ear canals and over his earlobes. "Now, what did you say?"

"The. Little. One. Is. Missing," she repeats, this time slower and louder.

"Good God almighty, why didn't you wake me?"

"He loves the bit of gardening," she directs her comment at us, "but it kills him at his age, and he needs his sleep. His health doesn't be great."

"I can hear you."

Paddy shoots me a look, and I know he will bring up her words later. He's never been happy with Christy doing our garden, claiming it was too much work for a man of his age, but recently changed to saying he gets a weird vibe from him, and he doesn't trust him. I suspect it's an awkwardness around Christy's hearing loss, too much of a reality mirror, but both Scarlett and I love the old man.

He always stays for a cuppa and a chat, and he's good to Scarlett, bringing her little bars and presents like the grandad she never had. He keeps our garden beautiful, but it has become secondary to his wonderful company or, dare I say, friendship. Neither Paddy nor I have a social circle anymore. Not like we used to. When I try to pinpoint the moment it happened, I can't. Work, then Scarlett coming, then her diagnosis, Paddy's promotions. Life just got busy, I guess, but apart from Jess, I don't have friends, and even she has her own life with work and her own family. Nobody has time for us anymore. Except Christy.

Mrs Devlin turns her face to Christy and speaks in a loud, slow voice. "There's – tea – in – the – pot."

"I don't want tea. Play that, will you?" She clicks the mouse, and the road, hedge and front gate appear on the laptop screen.

"Is this live?" Helen asks.

"It is," Mrs Devlin says.

Christy rubs his head. "I can't believe it. Scarlett, my little buddy."

"Can you show us earlier this evening, from about five o'clock?" Helen asks.

Mrs Devlin loads the file. Nothing passes until Paddy's black Mercedes speeds by the house towards ours. 6:27pm.

She replays it. This time Paddy drives by at normal speed.

"This is this evening?" Helen asks, and Mrs Devlin nods.

It's clear that Paddy is the sole occupant in his car. He appears agitated. She plays more footage. 17:00, 16:00. Nothing.

Paddy turns to me. "What time did you say you last saw Scarlett?"

"About half past five." He knows this.

"Would she have gone to see the sheep?" Christy asks, rubbing his watering eyes with a white hanky. "Or for a walk over the hills?"

"Yes, the fields," Mrs Devlin says, and I shake my head. "The ditches are overgrown with weeds. She's scared of nettles."

"Well, there is one thing for sure," Helen says. "Nobody passed by this house in the time frame we're talking about."

6

Mrs Devlin plays the footage from the beginning of the day. Paddy's car is first to pass coming from the direction of our house towards the main road at 6:31am. I recognise that face. He seems to be singing along with music from the car and looks bright for that time of morning. He used to look at me like that, a very long time ago, but now he reserves it for his real passion. Work.

"Can we go back to the footage from yesterday?" Helen asks.

Mrs Devlin clicks on Previous Day, and the footage runs from morning. Paddy leaving for work. When my 2009 red Opel Astra hatchback passes from the direction of our house, she pauses it. I'm in the front seat, driving, and Scarlett is in the back, looking out the window. I grip my chest. I don't even remember passing I was so deep in thought. Scarlett looks miserable, tracing her finger on the window.

Then images of nothing until evening when my car returns, travelling towards our house.

"Can you go back a bit?" Helen asks.

I drive by at 17:12. "There," Helen says. "Stop. Can you zoom in on the car?"

All eyes are on me now. The image of my car is large on the screen. Scarlett is not there.

"Scarlett's under that blanket. She took a lie-down on the way home from the zoo. It was busy and noisy, and we hit the rush hour traffic in Dublin. She was wrecked, so I told her to have a little rest."

Helen flips her notebook open and clicks her pen. "Where is the last place you saw Scarlett, Karen?"

I sigh. "Helen, I've answered that question already. It's getting dark outside, and we're no further along. What are you implying?"

"I'm implying nothing," she says before turning to Paddy. "When did you say you last saw Scarlett?"

"This morning."

"She was asleep, though? When you left?"

"Yes, I didn't want to disturb her. She's like a cat. The slightest thing wakes her up, and it was early."

"And you're sure she was in her bed?"

He rubs his chin. "Yes. I mean I didn't make sure it was her, that would be ridiculous, but someone was in her bed."

"This is ridiculous," I say. "She was in her bed. Stop asking stupid questions and get out and find my daughter."

Paddy gasps. "Karen!"

"No, Paddy, this isn't good enough. It's going to be pitch dark in the next hour, and we're still here, going around in circles, asking the same questions I answered earlier and going off on tangents. She's eight years old and somewhere out there. Have you forgotten her fear of silence and darkness, and that her batteries are dying? Look, I last saw Scarlett this afternoon in our house. She didn't go out the back gate, and now it seems she hasn't passed up this road, which means whatever has happened, she must be somewhere between our house and here. We should be combing every inch of the area. Why aren't we falling over ourselves to find her?"

I stop talking and catch a breath.

"She's right," Christy says. "We should be out there. I'll fetch my boots."

He squeezes my shoulder as he passes, and I pat his hand. "Thank you, Christy."

Helen continues to write.

"Helen, Scarlett was sleeping under that blanket on the back seat. Arrest me for my child not using a seat belt or a car seat, but otherwise can we get out there and find her?"

She stands. "Much obliged for your help, Eileen, Christy. We'll send for the CCTV footage."

"Least we could do," Eileen says. "I'll help with the search too." She walks us out through the kitchen and the back door as before, but Helen stays back, talking with Eileen. The dog raises her head but stays in the shade. As I walk through the yard, Paddy sidles up beside me.

"That was uncalled for," he spits, his gaze straight ahead.

I keep walking. "Scarlett is out here, Paddy. We know that now." I throw my arms out to the surrounding fields. "Here. And we're pissing around over her sleeping in the back of my car. You saw her yourself this morning."

We pass Helen's car, walk through the open iron gates and gather speed as we reach the lane. Twilight gives it a strange greyish hue, and all birdsong has stopped. The countryside astounds me how the wildlife beds in for the night. Scarlett should be too. Cuddling in with a bedtime story.

"Can I have the FM transmitter?" I ask him.

"Where are you going?"

"To find our daughter." I enable the flashlight on my phone.

He puts his hand on the transmitter. "Hold on, I'll come

too."

WE SEARCH bramble- and nettle-filled ditches along the lane, calling Scarlett as dusk descends. Tiny lights appear through the fields like a constellation of stars. Other people looking for my daughter or fireflies. I don't even know if fireflies exist in Ireland.

"Scarlett, come out. Game's over; you win. We give up," Paddy calls through the transmitter still hanging around his neck. I hold my phone out, praying it will connect to Scarlett's implants, when it rings.

My mother. I mouth "Mam" to Paddy. He rolls his eyes and walks ahead. My mother, Felicia Sullivan, is a straight shooter, but the most practical, clear-thinking woman I know, and I wish she were here; she'd know what to do. She raised me on her own while working two jobs to keep a roof over our heads. She raised me to be independent from before I started school.

When I gave up work to stay home with Scarlett after her diagnosis, my mother despaired of me. "I did not raise you to depend on a man," she said. "It's pathetic and weak." Pathetic and weak, the words of the woman who never told me who my father was, then married a millionaire and now lives in a mansion.

Paddy and my mother don't see eye to eye. He claims she's the most selfish woman he's ever met, taking off and leaving me to fend for myself at fifteen years of age. She says he's a selfish dweeb with peanut balls whom I settled for. At least they can be in the same room without killing each other, unlike me and Paddy's mother, Elenora O'Hara, the bitter old bitch.

I was five months pregnant when Paddy suggested I meet

his mother. My sickness hadn't subsided after twelve weeks as expected, and I had no choice but to take leave from work. All the way to her house in Skerries, I retched into the yellow basin on my lap, but Paddy drove the windy narrow roads hard regardless.

"I can't do this, Paddy. Bring me home and go yourself."

"She needs to meet the mother of her grandchild, Karen. It's not much further now, five minutes and we're there."

He drove into a small housing estate with a dozen detached houses arranged around a green space where children played, and stopped outside one of the larger houses. "Home sweet home. There's mother dearest."

A stern black-haired woman stood at the door, arms folded. "Welcome," she said, but the welcome didn't reach her face as she drank me in, inch by inch.

"Ma, this is Karen," Paddy said. I smiled and offered her my hand. "Pleased to meet you, Mrs O'Hara, Paddy told me all—"

"How long are you gone?" she asked, her eyes on my stomach.

"Um—"

Paddy put his arm around my waist. "Five months, Ma. You're going to be a granny. Isn't that wonderful news?"

"Hmm. Wonderful. Your dinner is on the table."

She turned on her heel and disappeared down the hallway. I grabbed Paddy by the shirt. "Did you not tell her I was pregnant?"

"No, she's set in her ways. I thought it was better if she met you first, got to know you."

"Jesus, Paddy! You should have told her before we came today. Now she hates me."

"Ma hates everyone."

The dinner was a feast for a king although it was technically lunchtime and there were only three of us there, one of us who couldn't eat. Roast chicken and ham, roast potatoes and parsnips, cabbage, carrots, stuffing and gravy. The smell of it alone made me want to run to the bathroom, but I managed to fight it.

"I assume you're going to marry *her*, then," Mrs O'Hara said, blanking me, while Paddy tucked into his food with relish.

"We haven't discussed that yet, Ma, with the babies coming, but maybe in time."

"Babies?"

"Twins."

She threw her napkin onto the table. "This just gets better. I despair of the young crowd today. Take the religion out of schools, out of hospital, out of life, and this is what happens. This."

My mouth moistened with sweat, and I burped. "I'm sorry, is there somewhere I can lie down? I don't feel well."

She rubbed her mouth with her napkin. "Patrick, show *her* to the guest bedroom."

After a detour to the bathroom to purge, I lay on the soft bed, glad to be out of that room. The pink and purple floral wallpaper matched the curtains, the fussy pelmets and the duvet cover. I closed my eyes to stop the visual onslaught.

When I woke, the light had waned, and I felt better than I had in months, before remembering where I was. Paddy's mother was horrid to me, but it must have been a huge shock to meet her son's girlfriend and discover she was going to be a granny to twins all in one day. No wonder she acted strangely.

I slipped out of the bed and onto the fuchsia carpet. Maybe if she got to know me, she'd see I wasn't so bad. I tiptoed down the stairs, stopping outside the kitchen door, where Paddy and his mother spoke in hushed tones.

"That woman has trapped you," she said. "How long have you been together?"

"A few months."

"Five?"

There was silence.

"My God, where did I go wrong?"

"Ma, don't say that. Is it because we're not married?"

"Oh, don't talk rubbish. It's because she's a slut. If she'll lie with you that quickly, she'll lie with others. You're still the fool you always were. Do you even know they're your babies?"

I tiptoed back up the stairs and to the bathroom, where I vomited violently. We left that evening, and I hadn't gone back since, not that she invited me. She refused our invitations too, feigning headaches.

When Paddy named our daughter Scarlett instead of Elenora, his mother called me for the only time in her life.

"Generations," she spat, "generations kept this tradition alive, and now you have ruined it all with your stupid name. Scarlett – what sort of ridiculous name is that?"

"Mrs O'Hara, it wasn't my idea to change the name."

"Rubbish. You're a gold digger, and that bastard child of yours will never be an O'Hara. Neither of you are welcome in my house until you put this right."

Paddy grabbed the phone from me. "We come as a package, Ma, and you don't get to say things like that to my family. Apologise to Karen now."

"Never."

We haven't spoken since.

"Karen, darling, are you there?" My mother's voice on the phone pulls me back to the lane and into the present. A couple of women pass by.

"Mam, where were you?"

"Resting. I wasn't aware I required prior permission," she barks, indignant as ever. "I woke to find nine missed calls from you. Where's the fire?"

How do I say her granddaughter is missing?

"Mam, something's happened. You might want to sit down."

"Oh, don't be dramatic, darling. Spit it out."

"Scarlett is missing."

There is a brief pause. "Since when?"

"Since this evening."

"Oh, Karen." Is she laughing or coughing? "That's hardly missing. Chances are she took a little stroll. You were always wandering off when you were seven years old, too."

"She's eight, Mam."

"Seven, eight. Same thing. It's the countryside, darling, she's supposed to explore. It's healthy."

A couple pass and nod to me, then another, and another. I don't think my mother is getting the severity of the situation. "Mam, there's an Amber Alert out. The Gardai are involved."

"I see." She lowers her voice. "Did you tell them about your marriage problems?"

"Mam!"

"Don't 'Mam' me. I told you it wasn't good for Scarlett to stay in an unhealthy environment. Children can sense tension, you know; it's why I never had a man around when you were growing up. The poor thing probably ran away; can't say I blame her."

"I have to go." I end the call and curse the Garda car that takes the corner too fast, almost running me over. I catch up with Paddy, and we search the ditches in silence until we see the flashing lights of patrol cars outside our house. As we approach, a small crowd gathered outside our house comes into view. I recognise some of them. It must be from events or their profile pictures when they interact with the Scarlett Hears page. Before.

Garda McCarthy climbs up onto the pillar at the front gate. "Folks, can I have your attention, please. As you know, little Scarlett O'Hara hasn't been seen since 5:30pm this evening. There are flyers here with her picture and description; please take one. We appreciate you coming out to help and will start a co-ordinated search at eleven. Please bear with us until then. Can we let the parents through?"

The crowd make way, and a Garda lifts the reflective yellow tape that stretches across the lane. Helen and I go inside, but Paddy goes back down the driveway to where Garda McCarthy now stands. They turn their backs and walk away, deep in conversation, the FM transmitter still around Paddy's neck. I think back to the last time Alex used it during a home visit.

Alex, Scarlett's speech therapist, arrived laden down with a speaker and, within minutes, had it plugged in and switched on. When Alex wore the transmitter, her voice came through the speaker, and Scarlett giggled. "I can hear it in my inside ears too."

"I have it set up to feed both into her implants and the speaker," Alex said. "It is great to create an auditory loop where she can hear her own voice back."

We had great fun doing karaoke with it. What if...? I switch on the speaker, and my husband's whisper comes through the speaker. I increase the volume.

"... it might be something. I don't know if I should even mention it. It's a long time ago."

I dash out to the front door. "Paddy, can you come here for a minute?"

He startles, like he's been caught with his hand in the cookie jar, but doesn't move. I wait for him, but my phone rings again, with an unknown number. I answer.

"Is this Karen, the mother of the child who is missing?"

"Speaking." I watch as Paddy comes back towards the house. Garda McCarthy keeps staring.

"Hello, I'm Fintan Power. You might have heard of me?"

"I haven't, no."

"I saw your plea on Facebook. I'd like to offer my professional services free of charge."

"Um, thank you... What is it you do?"

"I'm a psychic medium and a clairvoyant."

Helen is right, people are sick, and I've had enough for one day. "I'm hanging up—"

"No, wait, hear me out. This isn't a prank. There are police with you there, I can tell. Ask them about me."

I sigh. "What did you say your name was?"

"Fintan Power. I've worked with them before."

I mute my phone and go to find Helen, who is in the kitchen at the table on her tablet. "Fintan Power – you know him?"

"Yes, we know Fintan," she answers, not looking up.

"Is he legit?"

"He believes he is. He's been involved in a lot of missing persons cases."

"He's offering his services. Should I take him up on that?"

She shrugs. "Up to you. I wouldn't get your hopes up, but I can't stop you either."

"Do I get a say?" Paddy stands at the doorway. "I *am* her father."

"It can't hurt to let him help."

"It's wasting time, and it's bullshit."

I unmute the phone. "Fintan, we won't take you up on your kind offer yet, but you're very good to offer."

"I understand you might be reluctant, but I can help locate your Scarlett."

Paddy gestures to cut off the call and taps his watch. I grit my teeth. "You know what, Fintan, I would like that." I give him our address.

"Bullshit," Paddy repeats and stomps up the stairs.

7

"Fintan Power, pleased to meet you."

Barely fifteen minutes after he called, the clairvoyant is at the front door. I shake his hand and invite him into the living room. He is a short, grey-haired man with black-rimmed glasses and a pointy nose. Dressed in a khaki polo shirt and black jeans and carrying a black leather document holder, he is not at all what I was expecting. I offer him a seat, but he pushes his glasses up onto his nose and stays standing. Helen comes in from the kitchen.

"Hello, Helen," he says.

"Hello, Fintan," she says, sitting in an armchair.

"Now." He unzips his folder. "I'm here to help locate your daughter, so I'll have a look around, alright?"

Paddy comes downstairs and looks from Fintan to me to Helen, then raises an eyebrow.

"Fintan Power, pleased to meet you. I'm here to help locate your daughter."

Paddy folds his arms and stays standing. "Are you now? Can you tell us a little bit more about yourself, Fintan?"

Fintan blushes and shifts from foot to foot. "Oh, right. I

was born with psychic abilities, with a particular gift for locating people. I have been involved in many well-known cases, both here and in the UK."

Helen clears her throat.

"Like who?" Paddy asks.

Fintan pushes his glasses up his nose again. "Kasey Eyers, Jasmin Jones, Dermot Byrne to name but a few."

"And how does that work?" I ask.

"I channel their energy, and they guide me to their location. I'll get a feel for young Scarlett and channel her energy too." He walks around the room and stops in front of the framed picture on the wall, where Scarlett grins widely in a rubber ring.

"Is this she?"

"Yes, that's Scarlett. The picture was taken on our holidays two years ago in the pool in Torrevieja, so she's changed a little since then," I say. "Em, you said Kasey Jones?"

He moves to the shelf where Alex's speaker is and runs his hands up and down inches from the speaker. "I did, yes."

"Wasn't she the girl found dead in Cork?" I remember the case. She was eight years old, just like Scarlett, and taken from outside the school gate. Missing two weeks, she was found in Cork, locked in a shed and starved to death. Her abductor was returning from the supermarket with groceries when he was in a serious car crash and died.

"That's correct. And with my help, her body was returned to her parents. Jasmin and Dermot were alive. There's no time to lose."

I look to Paddy, and he sits down beside me on the sofa.

"Good. Great. First, I will pick up your energy, to eliminate it." He moves his hands over both Paddy and me and mutters something I can't make out. Then he goes out to the kitchen.

"This is ridiculous," Paddy spits and follows him out.

"It's worth a shot," I say to Helen. "What if he finds her?"

Helen shrugs. "Not my place to comment."

Fintan comes back into the room. "Where's Scarlett's bedroom?"

I show him to her room, where he examines every inch. "Does she have something special? Something that captures her spirit?"

"She has soft toys, but she really loves to paint." I offer him a brush from the cup on her desk.

"Perfect." Fintan takes a chain with a ring on it from his shirt pocket. He rubs the ring on the paintbrush and removes a large, folded sheet of paper from his bag. When he unfolds the paper, it's much bigger than I expected, and there isn't enough space on the floor to lay it down. "Is there somewhere better, bigger, to do this?"

Outside, it's completely dark when Helen and Paddy join us. I switch on the patio light and pull back our sun loungers to clear a space for Fintan to do his work. The noise of sirens and chatter from the lake and outside are like a midsummer party. A helicopter flies overhead. Maybe Paddy is right, this is wasting valuable time. I check my watch and want to vomit.

"Fintan, I don't want to be rude, but I'm going out of my mind here. It's a quarter to eleven, fifteen hours since her batteries were charged, and it's dark. Can you hurry up?"

Fintan unfolds the paper and lays it on the patio slabs. An enormous map of Ireland.

He stands in the middle of Ireland, right on Westmeath, and suspends the ring from the chain. "Scarlett, where are you?" The ring spins.

Paddy sighs.

"Scarlett, stop this ring spinning when I am close to you," Fintan says. He steps through the counties one by one, the ring spinning gently, but when he stands on County Sligo, to the west, it stops still.

I gasp. "She's in Sligo?"

Fintan steps off the map. "Scarlett, are you in Sligo?" The ring spins again. "Scarlett, stop this ring when I am close to you." The ring stops immediately.

He steps to his left and staggers backwards onto the white lounger. "There is a lot of energy here. Red. I'm feeling red."

Paddy tuts. "Her name is Scarlett, could that be it?"

Fintan opens his eyes and looks Paddy dead on. "No. A different red. Does that make sense?"

Paddy flushes and runs his fingers through his hair; he hates being wrong.

"Sligo," Fintan announces. He rifles through his bag before pulling out another map and laying it on the ground. An enlarged map of Sligo.

The ring stops dead over the west of Sligo. He drops it onto the map, and it lands in Enniscrone. "That's where I believe she is. On the beach. I'll go there right away."

"I'll let my colleagues know your findings. In the meantime, we'll join this organised search on the lake," Helen says.

Fintan folds his maps with care and precision. "I'll let you know as soon as I have anything."

I show him to the door. "Do you think she's okay?"

He looks to the ground. "Her energy is strong."

Paddy extends his hand, but he doesn't accept.

"That was interesting," I say as Fintan goes back to his car parked in the driveway. The crowds outside are building, and more police cars have arrived.

"That was bullshit. I'm going to the lake," Paddy says.

It's pitch dark and after eleven when we join the search on the lakeside. The shore is lit up with torches and lamps; the scene that greets us is incredible. People are everywhere.

Search and rescue patrol the lake, and sniffer dogs comb the shore. We can't enter the woods, as they comb them methodically. Groups with torches take direction from Gardai, who have stopped the press coming onto the lakeside.

The helicopter passes overhead. "It's equipped with thermal scanning," Helen says. "If she's in those woods, she'll be found."

Hours after I left the voice message, Jess calls back. "Karen. At last! I've been trying all night to reach you."

"Oh, Jess," I sob. "The signal is terrible here. I'm sorry."

"Jeez, Karen, no, don't apologise. I can't even imagine. Any news?"

"No, we're on the lake shore. Scarlett's missing."

"I know, I've been following it online from over here. I can't believe it."

My heart sinks. "You're abroad?"

"Yeah, Tenerife with the family. Of all the bloody times to go away."

The helicopter dips towards the centre of the woods, and Gardai radios echo with voices around us. Then they begin to move in that direction.

They've found something.

"Jess, I have to go. I'll call with any news." I end the call and run to the woods. The Gardai allow me to enter the darkness that reminds me of Dr Goldberg discussing her book on TV.

"Fairy tales are a fantastic way of teaching life skills while developing imagination," she said. "Take Hansel and Gretel. Siblings are stranded in the woods by their poor father and evil stepmother. The children outwit the adults by leaving a trail of stones for themselves and find their way back. The second time they are stranded, they take bread, leaving a trail of crumbs, which are eaten by the birds. Lost and scared, they fall prey to a kind old lady who lures them inside a gingerbread house with the promise of more treats and – spoiler alert – she's an evil witch who wants to eat them. This could be the start of a whole range of conversations about trust, lying, resilience, child safety and repercussions of actions. At each part of the story, pause and ask your child what they would do next."

"What sweets were on the house?" Scarlett asked when I read the story to her at bedtime a few weeks ago.

"The sweets were only to get them to come in." I pulled her into a cuddle. "Sometimes bad people pretend to be nice to trick you. What would you do if you were lost?"

She furrowed her brow. "There were no sweets?"

"There were but just to trick them. That's not what I'm asking you. If you were Gretel lost in the woods, what would you do?"

Her lip wobbled, and I regretted bringing up the subject, but then she licked her lips. "Can we get sweets tomorrow?"

I sighed and tucked her in. Her understanding was not there yet, but we could work on it. She gave me her implants to charge, and I kissed her goodnight, but as I left the room, she called after me, "Mammy?"

I stuck my head back in. "Yes?"

"I wouldn't be like Gretel because I wouldn't get lost."

I signed, "How?"

"I'd remember how I got there."

I kissed her, signed goodnight, and she signed I love you. Oh, what I would give to be back there again.

The helicopter leaves as word filters back it was a badger the thermal scanner detected in the woods, and the search is brought back out to the shore. News teams gather throughout the night; our narrow lane is lined with vans carrying equipment to broadcast our pain.

The Garda press office is handling communications. They said not to talk to anyone before the official media appeal at

9am. I have eighteen unread messages and countless missed calls. Helen warned me people want to help, and the vast majority won't be useful, but these calls are coming too fast to keep up, and the Wi-Fi out here is hit and miss, so they arrive in bundles. Finding a signal, I hop on Facebook Live. I can't answer all the calls and texts in a few minutes, but I can talk to the world through a live.

"Hi, guys. A quick update. We're on the lake. Still no sightings of Scarlett. I think a lot of you are here, much love for that. Please keep sharing her picture and contact the Gardai if you see her or if there's anything at all, or you can contact me directly. I'll try to answer as many messages as possible, but please bear with me. There is a theory that she might be in Enniscrone, and there is a search there, please join in or tell us anything you know. It's my baby girl, and her implants have been switched on over fifteen hours. She's so scared of the dark. Please help – imagine if it were your child. She should be home in her bed. She should be with us, her mother and father."

Paddy approaches, and I end the live broadcast. I turn in the opposite direction, afraid of what I will say to him. I am so annoyed with him for talking to Garda McCarthy earlier.

"Facebook again?" he asks.

My words spill out. "What were you going to tell Garda McCarthy before I called you in?"

His face drops. "Nothing. Why?"

I hold up the microphone hanging around his neck. "I heard you, Paddy. You swore you would never tell anybody what happened that day."

He pales. "Karen, I was worried, am worried. I thought that—"

"That I have something to do with this?"

"No, no, of course not, but..."

"But nothing. Do you think this is my fault? That's rich coming from you."

"You *were* with her last."

"Yes, I was with her. I'm always bloody with her because you're never home."

"Unfair. I do my best."

"You knew I was organising an important conference; you knew I was under pressure, and not once, NOT ONCE, did you offer to take time off or postpone your trip."

"It was important I went to London."

"So important the client cancelled" – I click my fingers – "at the drop of a hat."

"It wouldn't be the first time Scarlett's wandered off by herself."

"What are you talking about?"

"You know what I'm talking about. Last week, Tuesday, I think."

I was checking Eventbrite when Paddy pulled into the driveway, seething, with Scarlett in his passenger seat. He claimed he'd found her wandering up the laneway playing with "some fucking cat," which Scarlett had informed him was not "some fucking cat" but a pretty cat called Ginger, and she was not, in fact, wandering up the laneway but playing outside our house in the laneway.

"So you do think I'm to blame." He fidgets but doesn't answer me. "You know what, Paddy? You've some nerve. Just go. I can't be around you right now."

He leaves, and I cry again. How dare he accuse me of neglect after what happened to Hope because of his actions? How dare he after causing Scarlett's problems? Is it any wonder I suffered?

Night turns to morning, and the temperature rises with the sun. Searchers fall away, and someone brings soup and blankets to the lakeside. I sit on the end of the diving board, remembering my last counselling session with Brigid, my grief therapist, seven years ago.

"You've done amazing work here, week after week, Karen. How are you feeling?"

"So much better. I don't know if it's our sessions or the antidepressants, or both, but I feel much clearer and more than that. Hopeful."

Brigid sat listening, so I continued.

"I read somewhere a twin born who couldn't stay is called a sunset baby, and the surviving twin is a sunrise baby. I thought that was beautiful." I dabbed a tear. I was always crying in that room. It felt... right.

"When I found out I was expecting twins, I was devastated. My mother told me it was bad luck to buy anything before the babies came, which wasn't a problem for me because I was too depressed and sick to get out of bed. Paddy thought it was superstitious claptrap and said it was logical to get everything before they arrived. Moses' baskets, car seats, a double pram, baby shoes – he bought the lot. I never returned the extra set. I know I should have, but I guess as long as they're in the house, she's still with us, if that makes sense. Sometimes I still buy two of everything and hide one set."

Brigid sat back in her chair. "That makes perfect sense. Tease that out a bit, Karen. What do the objects represent to you?"

"I think if we can touch her things, it proves she was here; that if we let them go, she will fade, and one day I'll forget her." I sob. "But she was here – and she mattered. She mattered so much. I never got to meet her, and I will never forgive Paddy for taking that away from me, but I will always love her."

"Any update on the dangerous driving charge?"

"It's been dropped."

"You decided not to tell them about the phone, then."

"I don't have any fight left. Anyway, nothing will bring back Hope, so what does it matter?"

"Hope is a part of your family; she will always be with you. You don't need me to tell you that. Hope and Scarlett are twins, forever connected." She placed her hand over her heart. "She lives on in here."

We sat in silence, something I made my peace with in that room. She lit a candle and put it on the table.

"I read a six-word story," I said. "For sale: baby shoes, never worn. I think it was Ernest Hemingway. Isn't that sad?"

"The saddest. How are you doing with Scarlett?"

"I adore her, I do. She's incredible."

Brigid reached across the table and squeezed my hand. "So are you, Karen."

That evening, as I drove home into the vivid sunset, I felt a weight lift. I could never move on, but it was time to start living again for Scarlett's sake. I made a promise to myself: Scarlett would grow up knowing Hope, her sister, not from things bought but from stories we would tell. We would keep her alive in our words and our hearts. Hope would always have a seat at our table.

A gull swoops on the lake in front of me, catching a fish in its beak and bringing me back to this nightmare. We have to find her; there's no other option. I'll never survive losing another child.

Please help your sister, Hope, I pray, and my phone lights up with a call. It's Helen.

"We got CCTV footage from the zoo on Thursday. Come up to the house; we want you to take a look."

Thank you, Hope.

8

DAY 2 – 06:30

Missing 13 hours

It's strange walking into my house when other people are in it. A Garda stands in the hall, and Helen sits at the kitchen table with Paddy to her right. There's a free chair beside him, but I choose the one on the other side of Helen. He has some nerve making those comments, and I don't want to be near him for fear of what I might say.

There is a black tablet on the table in front of Helen. "My colleagues sent through the CCTV from the zoo where you or Scarlett are captured. If you see anything unusual, tell me." She presses play.

The entrance of the zoo appears on-screen, and Scarlett and I approach. I pay, and we enter. The view switches to the monkey enclosure, and after a few seconds we enter the shot. We chat and laugh, and then I reach for my phone. Scarlett is doing monkey impressions, but I've taken the call and have turned away. Her face drops.

Paddy shuffles in his seat, and I am relieved when the footage switches to the play area.

Swings, slides, sand, a merry-go-round and a climbing frame, the play area is packed with children of all ages flanked by coffee-carrying parents helping them. Scarlett runs straight to the slide and goes up and down it three times, interacting with children and adults and generally looking happy. I'm not in the footage because I was on the phone to Clonturk Castle, begging them to take the booking for Dr Goldberg, and they kept putting me on hold.

I enter the screen, phone to my ear, talking and gesturing. I talk to Scarlett, and she runs away from me. I follow her through the sand and grab her hand, but she swipes it loose and goes back up the slide. I try to coax her back down the steps when she turns and slaps me straight across the face. I yank her down from the fifth step, and she lands on the sand below. A woman stands open-mouthed, and a man shakes his head. Scarlett kicks and screams as I drag her out of shot.

Paddy gasps and covers his mouth as we leave the zoo, Scarlett now holding my hand and walking beside me, and the video ends.

"That's all we have," Helen says, not before time.

I couldn't bear any more. It's mortifying to see my actions on-screen, and heart-breaking to see Scarlett so small and fragile, but more than that, I don't have any memory of that incident or the reaction it elicited. None. I was engrossed in the call, in a different world, distracted. Those people in the play area had more time for my daughter than I had. Playing with her, talking to her, some adults who didn't even have kids with them.

Why would they be in the play area, then?

"Hold on. Helen, can you go back to the play area and play it again?"

Helen rewinds, and again, Scarlett plays on the slide, chatting with the other kids and parents who help their children up the steps and catch them at the bottom. A woman approaches Scarlett, helping her up the steps and catching her. Blonde bobbed hair, a little heavily built, dressed in a green top, baggy jeans and runners. I can't see her face, but she unnerves me, and I can't put my finger on why.

"What is it?" Helen asks.

"I don't know... can you play it one more time?"

The next time I get it. "That blonde woman who helps Scarlett on the slide doesn't have a child with her. Look, all the other parents are with children, but she's alone."

The wall facing us is covered with Scarlett's pictures, including one of Scarlett and Hope at the zoo on Thursday. I made dinner while she painted it.

Mammy, I had a great time with Hope in the zoo today.

–That's great, pet. Now, clear off the table and go get ready for dinner.

We're going to go to the beach next.

–That's nice.

Mammy, you're not doing good listening!

Then my phone rang, and I took the call in the garden. Keeping Hope's memory alive means we set a place for her at the table, put up a stocking for her at Christmas and celebrate both their birthdays. When Scarlett first said she sees her sister, it freaked me out, so I added play therapy to her already packed schedule. Her therapist was less worried.

Scarlett seeing Hope is a classic coping mechanism. For a little girl, she has been through a lot. Losing her twin sister, surgeries to hear, tunings, speech and language, the deafness itself and the recent house move. One of these events alone is huge in a child's life. If Scarlett sees Hope like an imaginary friend and that comforts her, I would let her have that. Most kids forget them once the trauma passes or when they make real friends. Don't worry, it's a phase that will pass, and if nothing else, it's a sign of a great imagination.

When Paddy came home from work that night, Scarlett

was asleep. I told him what the therapist said; he flipped. "We have to pretend Scarlett sees Hope for real? No way, I'm not going along with that."

"It's a phase that will pass; she's been through a lot."

"More like hippy-dippy claptrap. How much did I pay for that brilliant advice? Don't answer, it will make me even angrier. Look, she's a kid. Kids lie, it's their job to push boundaries, but we're her parents, and it's *our* job to push back. I'm calling her on it; how else will she learn? It will mess the kid up *even more* if we pretend to go along with this."

I examine Scarlett's hand-painted pictures on the wall through a new lens, a chilling theory developing further with every picture.

"What is it?" Helen asks.

The pictures have words scribbled in pencil at the bottom.

Hope and me at the zoo.

Hope and me in the park.

Hope and me at the pet farm.

Hope and me at the beach.

Deaf children can have difficulty imagining. They are quite literal if actions are not taken to override the language deficit caused by loss of incidental hearing, Dr Goldberg had claimed in her book.

"What is it?" Paddy asks. "Karen? What are you thinking?"

"Most of these places in the pictures we visited over the last few weeks, places I brought her so I could focus on organising this conference. Oh my God!"

I take a picture off the wall and put it on the table in front of them.

"What are we looking at?" Paddy asks.

"Hope is always blonde in Scarlett's pictures, right? On Thursday, when we came home from the zoo, Scarlett painted this one." I tap the picture. "She painted Hope with yellow hair, wearing a green top and blue trousers. Now look at the woman in the zoo. She's blonde and has a green top and jeans. They're the same person. Scarlett told us she plays with Hope, she sees Hope, she talks to Hope. She never once said she *imagines* Hope; they were our words. What have we done?"

"Have you lost your mind?" Paddy says.

"Look. At. All. The. Pictures. I knew Scarlett wouldn't go with anyone unless she knew them."

"But you were with her at all those places; you would have noticed someone talking to her."

I ignore his comment. "Can you play it one more time, Helen? Please."

We watch again as the woman interacts with Scarlett, but then she helps another child and another. Her face is concealed.

"She acts the same with all the kids," Paddy says. "Maybe she's an aunt or a friend of a child there. Or maybe her own child is out of shot."

I shake my head. "No. Look how familiar Scarlett is with her. She wouldn't be so at ease unless she knew her."

"Which means what?"

"Which means Scarlett knows this woman as Hope. She's been telling us about her, painting her, meeting her, and we dismissed it all as fantasy. This woman has groomed our daughter and taken her from under our eyes."

9

ELAINE

Twelve months ago

"After the break we will be joined by Karen O'Hara, whose experiences following the birth of her daughter, Scarlett, have the nation talking. Stay with *Good morning, Ireland*."

A lump of grey porridge falls from Daddy's flaccid mouth and onto his spiky chin. I catch it with a tea towel before it drips onto his bedsheet.

"Yes, that does sound interesting, Daddy."

The doctors say they don't know how bad the brain damage is following the stroke, but I chat away to him regardless. It's company for me too, with just the two of us here. My routine since I came back to Ireland is cooking, cleaning and taking care of my father. I thought my life would look different at forty; I thought I would be married with children, but it was not to be, which worked out in Daddy's favour since the added cancer diagnosis. The doctors said to cherish every moment; I haven't left his side.

I hold his head up and plump his pillows, the greasy

imprint on the cream pillowcase reminding me to include it in the wash later. I prop him up as the upbeat familiar music heralds the morning show's return.

"Here we go, Daddy." I take my place in the wooden armchair beside his bed and turn up the volume on the old TV that sits on the mahogany dressing table at the foot of his bed.

The presenter smiles to the camera; her black bob as sharp as her white shirt. "Welcome back. I'm Sally David, and this morning I am talking to mother and blogger Karen O'Hara, whose vlog went viral earlier this week. Welcome, Karen."

Karen O'Hara is stunning. Her long blonde hair falls in tousled curls past her perfect face and down her tanned shoulders. She wears a black shift dress that hugs every curve, and her long legs are complemented by ruby red stilettos. Stunning.

Daddy grunts again.

"She is gorgeous, you're right, Daddy."

I catch my reflection in the mirror of the dressing table, my scrubbed hands twisting the pendant on my gold necklace. I sit up straighter, fixing my shapeless mustard sweater. I dress for the job I have, not the one I want, and this is my lot. Besides, Mammy always said it's what's on the inside that counts.

Last December, I celebrated my fortieth birthday here, me and Daddy. Coming back home allowed me to shut the world out.

London was an escape, but that version of me wasn't sustainable. When living a lie, the turmoil is too much, and something has to give. This is me, the true me, dowdy and forgotten. The person I was supposed to be. Daddy was right, I didn't amount to much. I baked a chocolate sponge for my birthday and lit my own candles. I put a party hat on

Daddy's head and sang "Happy Birthday" to myself. It was grand.

On the TV, Karen flashes a dazzling smile, displaying perfect white teeth. "Delighted to be here, Sally."

"Karen, could you take us back to the now-famous post and tell us what happened?"

I spoon porridge into Daddy's mouth while keeping my eyes on the screen.

"Sure, Sally," Karen says. "When I first became a mother, I suffered from postpartum depression. I didn't realise what it was at the time; thought it was a normal way to feel."

"How did it manifest itself, Karen?"

She crosses her long legs. "It's still hard to say this, but I never wanted children. All women are supposed to want them, right? It's what we're told from when we're little girls and encouraged to play with prams and dolls. Not me, I never wanted to be a mother. Looking back, I think the depression developed early in my pregnancy. I felt so helpless, I hated what my body was doing and that I had no control over myself anymore. Add to that my hyperemesis gravidarum."

I stop feeding Daddy and turn up the volume.

Karen brushes a curl back with long tanned fingers, their nails painted red. "I had my whole life planned out. I was going to be CEO one day, and my hard work was paying off. Within one year, I was due for another promotion, when I fell pregnant unexpectedly. I developed hyperemesis gravidarum, basically morning sickness but twenty-four seven for nine months. I was devastated, but the world continued without me, and I felt forgotten. I don't know if it was depression or exhaustion, but I toppled into the deepest hole."

Daddy gags. I take the water bottle from the tray on the bedside locker and push the straw from it between his dry cracked lips. "I know, Daddy. Some people have no idea how lucky they are, do they?"

"Then, at twenty-six weeks pregnant, there was the car accident that left me in a coma for three weeks."

Sally pats Karen's hand. "That's terrible."

"I recovered well, but my babies weren't so lucky. Scarlett's prematurity led to complications, and the drugs they used to save her life most probably caused her deafness. She had a twin sister, Hope; her lungs weren't strong enough, and unfortunately, she passed away at three days old, meaning I never got to meet her. All of this didn't – couldn't – have helped."

The presenter tilts her head in sympathy. "It's a lot for anyone to deal with. Your husband, Paddy, it was he who noticed your depression, right?"

A portrait of the couple appears on-screen, and Paddy is absolutely average. Where she's a strong eight out of ten, he's barely a four. "Someone is punching above their weight, eh, Daddy? No need to ask if the husband has money."

Karen's smile drops. "There he is."

"Is he watching from home this morning?" Sally asks.

"No, he's at work." Karen tucks her hair behind her ear. "He's a partner in ICT Technologies, where we both met. He works hard to take care of our little family."

Sally talks to the camera. "For the viewers at home, we asked him to come on, but—"

"He's quite private," Karen says.

"I'm sure he's delighted with his wife airing all her dirty laundry on TV so," I say to Daddy.

The presenter leans forward. "You went to see the doctor, is that right?"

Karen exhales. "Yes, that's correct. Paddy was worried about me, said I had become thin and withdrawn. At the time, I wasn't sleeping or eating, and recently I saw a picture of myself from that time. He was right. I was a wreck. He badgered me until I went to see the doctor."

Nice to have someone to care.

"I didn't want to admit I needed help," Karen continued. "What kind of mother was I? I wanted to be better, but I was so very tired."

A picture of a baby with brown curls, ocean-blue eyes and long eyelashes fills the screen. The most beautiful baby I have ever seen, and my heart leaps.

"There she is. Oh, gosh, that's an old picture." Karen lights up.

The presenter nods. "It all came to a head one morning seven years ago. Tell us about that."

"It was a January morning when I went to see the doctor. I hadn't slept in days, maybe weeks. I walked for hours and came home to Paddy in tears, admitting I couldn't continue like that. Admitting I needed help."

"That took a lot of courage. Did you get support?"

Karen takes a sip of water from the glass on the table in front of her. "Yes. Counselling, antidepressants, which I am still on and probably will be for life, and an acknowledgement it wasn't my fault. I made the vlog to talk about it and to try to reduce the stigma for any mums out there struggling like I was."

Sally clears her throat. "You run a social media page called Scarlett Hears, documenting Scarlett's journey. Do you find this cathartic?"

"Extremely so, Sally. It keeps me busy but also makes me feel like I am making the world a better place."

Grandiose or what?

"Karen, our time has almost come to an end. I've enjoyed our chat today so much I feel like we could talk for hours. To finish up, if there is someone at home who is suffering right now, what should they do?"

She flutters her long, fake eyelashes. "There is nothing to be ashamed of. It's not your fault. You are not mad or bad if you're struggling, you are simply human. Talk to someone; there is help."

"Great advice," Sally says as Karen sips her water, then almost as an afterthought asks, "How is Scarlett doing now?"

A photo of a little girl fills the screen as Daddy breaks into a fit of coughing.

"Oh, Sally, she's great," Karen says. "She was diagnosed as deaf as a baby, but strange as it sounds, that wasn't as traumatic for me as not wanting her."

I gasp in synchronisation with the presenter. The camera moves in for a close-up of Karen, who smiles, seemingly oblivious to what she just said.

"Eh, eh, right. Well, um, thank you for joining us, Karen, and for your candidness. We have to go to a break, but if you at home have been affected by this piece, the numbers of support services are appearing on your screen now and are listed on our website and socials."

The music and graphic of the show play. I switch the TV off, trying to process what happened. The stupid woman doesn't know how lucky she is to have a child. What I and thousands, maybe millions of women would give to be in her position! I rub the miniature footprint on my pendant. Emily.

10

ELAINE

Five years ago

I'm early for my pregnancy scan. The train arrived into Heuston Station, Dublin, on time for once, so I decide to walk the three kilometres there instead of taking my usual taxi ride. The sun warms my skin as I ramble down the quays along the River Liffey. A wonderful midsummer's day, tourists stop to take photos, and the air is alive with hope. I pull into the Jervis shopping centre to use the toilet. I could pee in a teacup at this point but still constantly need to go with baby pressing on my bladder.

I check my underwear for blood when I finish weeing, an action that is terrifying but necessary. Clear. Phew! This isn't my first pregnancy, but it's my longest. Right from the start, before fish smelled too fishy, before my boobs inflated, before that telltale exhaustion, I knew. This time is different.

At twenty-six weeks pregnant, and over the danger period of fourteen weeks, I should be able to relax, but I won't; not until the baby is here. I'm no stranger to the elation of a positive pregnancy test followed by the dread of cramps or blood spots signalling the end of the dream. I have lived like this for over two years, yet this horrendous, expensive, painful journey called IVF with sperm donation will be worth it. I'm going to fulfil my destiny to be a mother if it kills me.

I adore children, having worked with them since forever, but the endless stream of pregnant mums followed by new babies in the nursery is cruel. Families of two or three little ones announcing their family is expanding when all I need is one. One baby to love. One baby to make me a mother. I finish in the toilet and wash my hands, careful to clean them properly, then dry them in the air dryer. I appraise my growing bump in the full-length bathroom mirror and can barely hold in the joy. I look pregnant. Not overweight or a little lumpy, but for the first time, I have an undeniable bump.

"When are you due, love?" an old lady asks from the handbasin behind me.

I hadn't noticed her come in.

She blushes. "I'm sorry, I hope I didn't put my foot in it. You are pregnant, aren't you?"

"You didn't. I'm twenty-six weeks." I rub my bump.

"Oh, thank God. I never know if I should say anything to a lady like yourself in case it's just fat, but I think it's a wonderful thing."

"Not at all. I'm over the moon with this little miracle."

Five cycles of IVF it took to make this happen. This is my last chance. IVF is gruelling, emotional and exhausting, but that is not the reason I have to stop. I'm almost broke. Very little left in the bank, and you need money to raise a child.

In the main concourse of Jervis shopping centre, I am passing by the enormous window of Mamas and Papas towards the exit when the most beautiful cradle catches my eye. A traditional white wicker basket with purple flowers, set on a rocking base. €499 the price tag says. It won't hurt to look; I can't afford it, anyway.

"It's lovely, isn't it?" the young shop assistant says from behind me. The baby-powder scent of the lining adds to its soft beauty.

Could I buy it?

I tear myself away and finger the New Baby clothing in blues, pinks and pastels instead. I'm glad I don't have money. If I did, I would buy the lot, and I can't afford to tempt fate. Mammy always said buying things for babies before they're born is bad luck.

To my right, a heavily pregnant woman with a toddler in a buggy and an older lady coo over a pink vest with the words "Grandma's Gorgeous Girl." I wish my mother were alive; she would be here with me today. By the time I arrive at the Dublin Maternity hospital, I'm forty-five minutes late and have missed my appointment. Through a tightened jaw, the young receptionist informs me I will be seen as soon as they can fit me in.

In the waiting room, loved-up couples come and go, fawning over each other, while I wait. One hour and twenty-three minutes later, I take my place on the paper-lined black leather bed, supporting my head with my hands, as the sonographer spreads cold gel on my bump. I adore it, delighted to swap my jeans for loose maternity clothing.

The sonographer runs the camera over my tummy, and we both watch the monitor to my left. Then again and again.

"Love, is there someone with you?" she asks.

"No, I'm doing this all by myself," I say, dampening a rising unease. She could ask that question for any number of reasons; it doesn't have to be the worst-case scenario. Maybe she's annoyed with me for being late for the appointment, or she's supposed to be on her lunch break. "Train was late; sorry for keeping you."

"No worries," she says, concentrating on the screen and pulling the camera over my belly. She drags the camera down to my pelvis and pushes it in hard to my full bladder.

Thump. Thump. Thump.

"There you are," she says.

"There you are!" I cry to the silhouette of a tiny human on the screen, kicking away. I wipe the tears from my eyes and laugh. "You're a kicker like your daddy."

She laughs. "Dad's a footballer?"

"Yes. Dad's a donor who is a footballer."

She rubs my arm. "Would you like to know the gender, love?"

I pull myself up on the bed to get more comfortable. "Yes, I think so, although I don't mind as long as it's healthy."

That's what I say when anyone asks, and it is true, but if I *had* to choose, I would love a little girl. A girl I can share all the moments I never got to share with my lovely mother. First bra, first period, first baby. Yes, a girl would be nice, but either would be cherished.

"Are you ready to find out?"

"Born ready." She moves the camera further down my bump until the baby's lower abdomen is on the monitor. She clicks the keyboard beside her, and the picture freezes.

"Mamma, get ready to have a baby girl."

That's when I lose it. Years of loss, pain, disappointment and fear fall away, and in their place rush relief, happiness and hope, with the overwhelming emotion of love. I am going to have a baby girl.

I leave the hospital gazing at the printed scan. "Hello, Emily Murtagh. A special name after a special lady for a special little girl." I didn't opt for the genetic testing, unwilling to disturb that safe amniotic bubble, and besides, I will love her no matter what challenges she might have. I will love her every moment of every day of her life. I already do. I hail a taxi to take me to Heuston train station and sit in the front seat.

"I'm having a baby girl," I tell the taxi driver, a Dublin man in his sixties.

"Good for you, love. Now, where are we heading?"

Walking along the platform at the station, something is off. It starts with a dragging in my lower stomach, and then a mind-blowing cramp stalls me mid stride, followed by a gush of wetness. A man in a suit on his mobile phone walks along the platform towards me and glances down at my trousers. His hand flies to his mouth. I follow his gaze to see what I already know. My white trousers are splattered with fresh red blood.

———

THE DELIVERY IS BEYOND TRAUMATIC. Fast and intense, with nobody to hold my hand. At 15:52pm on July 13, with one final excruciating push, Emily Murtagh is born weighing two pounds and one ounce. Silent. I put my arms out to hold her, ready for the skin-to-skin contact I've studied, ready to breastfeed, ready to do anything for my girl, but she's hurried to the neonatal ward amidst whispering and worried faces.

When I stop haemorrhaging and I'm cleaned up, they wheel me to her incubator in the neonatal ward, where wires run from her, and machines beep around her. She is perfect.

If she makes it through, I will spend every moment of my life loving her.

Please, Mammy, God and the angels. Please don't take her.

The beeping from the machines increases until it is a continuous tone. Doctors rush in. So many doctors. "You need to leave."

Wires, tubes, orders I don't understand.

The tone continues. "You need to leave. Now."

For the next hour, a nurse comforts me outside the door until doctors leave the unit, one by one, not making eye contact. An older doctor approaches and takes off her glasses. "I'm so sorry. We did all we could."

They wrap her in a pink blanket and let me stay with her all night. I smile through the agony for photos of the two of us, and they take impressions of her little hands and feet. They said some bereaved parents like me take comfort from having memorials made from them.

Five days later, I leave the hospital, heartbroken but otherwise as I arrived, empty-handed. A week later she is buried. Ballygrave funerals are usually massive, but this time it is just Father Kelly and me. I don't want Daddy here, and I didn't tell anyone else; people will be awkward, and I've been gone so long.

Emily is buried in the "Grandma's Gorgeous Girl" pink Babygro in the white wicker basket with the purple flowers that smells like talc beside Mammy in our family plot. It's tragic and beautiful. Mammy, who went to mind the angels, now has her own grandchild to care for who carries her name.

There is no meal and no drinks afterwards. No words of condolence. Daddy stays out of my way on the farm, and the next day I get the train back to Dublin. Life is supposed to return to normal, but for the first time in my life, I can't get out of bed. I've always kept going through the hard times, but what difference do I make to anybody? The results of Emily's post-mortem come back as inconclusive. It's all pointless.

When I run out of sick notes and the bills mount up, I return to work in the nursery. The staff say the strangest things to me, and they're the ones who say anything at all. Others ghost me, avoid me, freaked out by the woman whose baby died like it's contagious. My colleagues were shocked when I announced my pregnancy. They joked they didn't even know I had a fella. Going back is hell on earth, surrounded by babies and children, but I need the money, and I'm not qualified for anything else.

"You can try again," a co-worker says. "When you heal, you can get back on the horse." She doesn't know about the IVF or the sperm donation. Nobody does; it's not their business.

I'm like a pariah in the canteen. What do you say to such a woman as me? Do you call her "the baby" or by her name: Emily? What if you say the wrong thing? These are questions I wish I didn't learn the answer to. I wish they asked me because I would say please talk to me, please ask me, I want to talk about Emily. For a short time, she was here as much as you are. She existed.

When I think life can't get any worse, the bleeding starts again, and this time it doesn't stop. Cancer comes to kick me when I'm down and leaves with my ovaries. They take my womb out too, just to be safe. This time I don't go back to work. Instead, I buy a one-way ticket to London.

11

ELAINE

Day 1 – 05:15

I throw back the blanket on my single bed, draw the heavy floral curtains and open the top window. The sun is rising, the busy birds filling my bedroom with their song. I look out to the forest, deep green and inviting, when a tiny bird slams hard into the window and drops to the ground, where a black cat waits. I shout at the cat to scram, but it ignores me and tosses the bird into the air. I peek into Daddy's room when I pass. He's still sleeping, which is unusual, but I won't look a gift horse in the mouth on such a wonderful day. I boil the kettle on the stove and make a flask of instant coffee to take with me to the woods.

Outside in the cool morning, I snip red roses from the garden once Daddy's pride and joy but now neglected and overgrown. The roses still bloom every year; they still return no matter what.

I enter the familiar woods. Here and there a glimpse of sunlight pierces the trees, creating warm corridors as I trek up the hill. This forest is my haven, my home. I know every inch of this land, every twist and turn. I could sleepwalk through it and still find my way.

I had been sleepwalking through my life since I returned to Ireland but woke up the day Karen O'Hara went on TV. Her Facebook page Scarlett Hears that she mentioned that day has every detail of their life, every place they visit, and it's all public. No need to friend, like or follow.

She doesn't know anything about me. I am a literal stranger.

The day I went to the park was a trial. I stayed a safe distance away, disguised in a blonde wig and oversized clothing, feeding the ducks. I brought the wig home from London; it had a special place in my heart, having got me through chemotherapy three years ago. The cancer wouldn't leave without a fight.

Karen posted all their plans with plenty of notice. How stupid can you be? Anyone could be watching, yet they were alone here in the park. That was strange.

Scarlett wore a darling baby pink dress and kicked a football with little white runners while Karen was all Mrs Important, chatting on her phone. Tall and slim, she was even more beautiful in real life and taller than I expected. With her oversized sunglasses, she rocked her skinny jeans and Converse, a popular girl in school, no doubt. The type who flushed my books down the toilet and called me names. School was tough, but it was preferable to staying home. With him.

I hadn't intended to talk to Scarlett that day, but when her ball bounced down to the lake and landed beside me, I picked it up and handed it to her.

She thanked me in the cutest voice. I wanted to throw my arms around her and shower her in love, but I let her run back up to the play area, to Karen, who was still on her phone.

Through Karen's Facebook updates on where they would

be, I continued to monitor the child from a distance and in disguise. I felt better knowing she was okay, and she had someone who gave a tuppence about her, even if she didn't know it. I only ever wanted the best for her, even if her own mother would prefer if she were never born.

The Facebook page was such an insight into Karen's thoughts. It was fascinating how she handled the passing of Scarlett's twin sister, Hope. Karen talked about her in the present tense, as if she were still here, not an angel in heaven, not dead. Still here. All I did was monitor, blend, watch until that day, the day that changed everything nine months ago.

Belvedere House and gardens is where Karen said they'd be. In a woolly hat, coat and sunglasses, I arrived ten minutes early and took up position at a picnic table with a clear view of both playgrounds. Karen and Scarlett arrived bang on time. Karen surveyed around her, looking for company no doubt, but as usual, there was none. Camouflaged by shrubbery, I was enjoying watching Scarlett in a pink rain jacket and jeans as she ran from one playground to the other when I copped Karen coming straight towards me. I dived down, rummaging in my tote bag, my heart thumping, but she passed on by. I waited a few moments, then sat back up to find Karen had joined the long queue at the coffee kiosk.

I envied her so much in her leather biker jacket and tight jeans. Why did she get to be a mother? She didn't even appreciate it. I looked back to the playground where Scarlett had been playing last and then to the other. The child was gone.

Nowhere to be seen, not the slides, swings, picnic benches. Nowhere.

Karen moved up one place in the kiosk queue. Both playgrounds swarmed with excited children, but Scarlett was not in either. Maybe she was in the twisty tube slide out of view. A child climbed the ladder, disappearing through the tube slide and reappearing at the bottom. She was not in there.

Karen turned towards the closest playground, her large sunglasses covering her eyes, but the barista called for the next customer, and she went to the counter.

A hedge-lined tar path sloped downhill to the open lake shoreline. With trembling hands, I packed up my things and strolled towards the lake nonchalantly so as not to attract attention. This was risky. Months of work could be destroyed in one careless move, but I couldn't sit by while something happened to Scarlett. I would never forgive myself.

Halfway down the hill, I spotted her throwing stones at the shoreline. Alone.

Thank God.

Nestled in the trees, a vacant picnic bench to my left offered an ideal viewing point, and I was settling in to watch her when a middle-aged man came from the bushes to the left and glanced around before bending to talk to the child. The way he put his hand on her back made my skin crawl. I leapt to my feet and marched towards them, phone to my ear.

"Yes. Hi, Mary, how are you? Out here in Belvedere. It's beautiful. Yes, I'm just by the lake." I was loud; risky, but I didn't care.

"Hello," I said, eyeballing him on my approach. "Lovely day." I stopped metres away from Scarlett and the man, still talking on my phone but staring at him until he slithered away in the direction he came.

"Hi." She was beside me. "What's your name?"

"Scarlett? Where are you?" Karen called from the top of the hill. I winked at the child and continued on the path and into the gardens, still talking on my phone.

I rested by a sculpture of Archangel Gabriel standing tall amongst the multicoloured flowers, struggling to process the implications of what had almost happened. If it weren't for my intervention, she'd have been taken. That was nine months ago, and how things have worked out.

I exit the woods by my home at the top of the hill after a brisk ten-minute walk and climb to the pinnacle. I survey the countryside below me; six counties visible from here, nothing but green. Through the broken iron gate of the graveyard lies my mother, her grave marked by a white wooden cross.

Emily Murtagh
1956–1989

The roses in the glass vase on her grave have shrivelled. I reach in, my hand catching in a web full of dead flies, and squash a spider as it tries to escape. I rinse my hands with water from my backpack and half-fill the vase with the remaining water. As I place the fresh roses into the vase, a large black earwig crawls out of one of the flowers and down the vase.

The small mound beside Mammy's grave makes a perfect resting place, and I pour two coffees into the white plastic flask mugs, placing one beside the cross.

"Bottoms up, Mammy."

I swipe my phone to unlock it. There's no Wi-Fi in the house, and 4G is patchy in Ballygrave. The best spot is here, at the top of the hill, where I have spent hours downloading Karen's videos ready to watch and rewatch into the night.

There is a new post on the Scarlett Hears page.

"Hi, Hearoes. Karen here. Crazy excited about my meeting with Dr Goldberg this evening at six. Almost there, lots to discuss. I can't believe this is happening. Better get some sleep. #BestDayEver #Eek #FairyTales."

After a tidy-up of Mammy's grave and a little prayer, I return to the house, the sour stench hitting me the moment I open the back door. Daddy. I change him, his eyes sad while I keep an upbeat chat about something and nothing going. I settle him back into bed and kiss his forehead.

"Now, Daddy, it's time for *Heartbeat*. You love that one."

His eyes follow me as I turn on the TV. "I'm going out for the day; I won't be back until late."

He cries out.

"I have to have a life, Daddy. Don't worry. I'll make sure you're well looked after before I leave. I'll give you something to help you sleep."

He yelps, his arm falling out of the bed. I tuck it back in. "No, Daddy, don't upset yourself. I have it all figured out."

His eyes close.

"Be like that. I'll be back later. Don't worry about me."

That makes me laugh, and once I start, I can't stop. I hold on to the bedpost to stop falling over.

"Ha, ha, ha. Worry about me. That's a good one."

12

ELAINE

Day 1 – 19:00

The key to rescuing a child is planning, pivoting and patience.

I didn't know when I woke up this morning that today would be the day, but I was prepared for plan B. I'd researched CCTV along the route and had planned alternative exits in case of emergency. Scarlett was ready. We both were.

Hiding in the long grass, and at times in plain sight, is key to success, so blending is an essential skill. It takes a lot of effort to become so average you're invisible, but it is possible and necessary. All the times I met Scarlett, nobody saw me. Even when she told them about me, they still didn't. That was no accident.

This evening, Scarlett came with me, through her back gate and onto the lake shore of her own free will. Wearing the baseball hat, navy sandals and blue T-shirt I brought, we chatted as we made our way along the lake shore. One of a hundred families going to a hundred cars in the packed car park on a sunny summer's day. All average. Nothing to see here.

Playing the long game takes patience. Building trust with the child pays off but takes time, with pivoting a vital skill. Children crave human connection, and Scarlett was crying out for attention, for validation. Her father was never around, and her mother may as well have been absent, such was her interest. Scarlett was looking for someone to love her. She was looking for me.

Even though there are millions of children in the world, the right child finds you. Scarlett is special. In the back seat of my car, she chatted while I drove out of the car park and away from the lake. She was so excited about our trip to the beach that I knew I had done the right thing bringing her. It was a pity it had to happen like this, but that wasn't my fault.

We passed an ice-cream van with a long queue at the side of the road. "Can we get ice cream?" she asked.

"Later, sweetie. I have lots of sweets in my picnic basket in the boot. I'm excited about our trip to the beach. Are you?"

"Yippee. I told my Mammy I'm going. I brought my swim-suit." She holds her T-shirt up to reveal a pink and purple striped one-piece.

My heart skips a beat. "You told your mother you're coming? What did she say?"

"She said that was nice."

I slap my forehead, and Scarlett laughs. "Oops, silly me, I forgot my swimsuit. We'll take a quick stop at my house and get it first."

She didn't worry as we drove up rural roads and around the back of the house.

She knew the house from the photos I showed her many times. Preparing a child is vital to minimise variables, Karen said on one of her many vlogs. I had prepared her well.

Scarlett didn't blink when I drove my '07 silver Avensis into the garage and locked the door.

"Oh, stinky," she squealed when I opened the back door of the house.

"My poor daddy. He's not well," I told her. "Maybe I'll clean him up before we go to the beach."

"Poo." She held her nose.

I bent down to her eye level. "I'll tell you what, I'll show you the secret room I made for you, and you can play while I clean him up. Then we'll go to the beach."

She scrunched her nose as if to object but then nodded. I guided her to the room in the basement, and she hesitated at the doorway but then stepped through. Her face lit up. A bed with a pink duvet cover and pillowcase sat against the far wall, and butterfly motifs peppered the white walls. LED lights twinkled and changed colour on the white ceiling. She ran to the table where I had laid art materials and then to the disco ball in the other corner. When she became engrossed in changing the colours on the lights, I eased out of the room, closing the door behind me.

My own little girl at last, here, just like I dreamed of. Mammy always said I would make a great mother.

Mammy. Before she got sick, she was gorgeous and fun and funny and lovely. She could light up a room with her smile. Everyone said it, but she only had eyes for me. She was a large woman, in stature and weight, and that made her great for cuddling. She always wore a primrose yellow pinafore, or pinny, as she called it, and danced around the kitchen while cooking or cleaning. She would take me by the hands and twirl me around, her thick auburn hair flying behind. Then Daddy would come in with mucky boots and a scowl and suck the joy out of the room. She'd return, in silence, to washing the dishes.

An avid reader, she always had a book in her hand. She

read everything she could get her hands on from Mills and Boons to Maeve Binchy, from Agatha Christie to Edgar Allan Poe. Other people had televisions but not us. It was all books, and I couldn't have been happier sitting by the fire, embraced in this serenity. She brought me to the library every week, and we always returned with a huge heist.

One day, she beckoned me to sit on her lap. I was engrossed in the fictional girls' boarding school of Enid Blyton's Malory Towers. She was my favourite writer, and I didn't want to put it down, but when Mammy called me again, I put my bookmark on the page and went to her.

She took me onto her lap and rubbed my head. "Lainey, I have something to tell you. I'm sick again."

I whipped around to see her face and didn't need to ask any more. "It's not fair," I cried. "It's not."

"I know," she said, holding me tighter and covering me in kisses. "I know."

In no time, she was skin and bone, her beautiful auburn hair all gone. Too weak to read herself, I narrated books to her after school and my chores. The librarian let me take as many books as I wanted, and I tried to choose books Mammy liked, but the words were too hard, so I borrowed children's books too.

She loved me reading to her, and even at the end, when she had her eyes closed and couldn't hear me, I still read. My chores got harder and longer. Someone had to do the house-keeping while Daddy worked on the farm.

Whenever there was bad news, neighbours descended on the house and talked in hushed tones. That was what happened the day Father Kelly called.

I made a pot of tea and poured it into a china cup kept for important visitors. I buttered some soda bread and gave it to him on his knee in the sitting room beside the turf fire.

He took a large bite of the thick bread. "Now, Elaine, your

mother is going to heaven." His stubby finger stuck out from the little china cup as he sipped his tea, and my world ended.

Don't cry. Be brave.

Big, stupid, betraying tears rolled down my face.

He patted his black comb-over. "Now, Elaine, there is no need to get upset. Your mother is a good Catholic. She has suffered in grace and always kept her faith. God will take her to heaven. We should rejoice."

I knew I wasn't supposed to answer a priest back, but I couldn't help it. "I don't want her to go to heaven."

"God needs her to mind the angels."

"Stupid angels. They can't have her; she's my mammy. I love her, and I need her. She's mine. Let them get their own mammy." I ran out of the room and up the stairs, burying my head in my pillow.

Three nights later lots of people called to see Mammy, but I wasn't allowed to leave my room. I read a whole book I got for Mammy that night.

Early the next morning, Daddy knocked on my bedroom door. "Elaine, your mother is gone to heaven. Get dressed and come downstairs."

I cried and cried, cursing God and heaven. I had to see her. When the coast was clear, I sneaked down the three steps from my room, onto the landing, across the creaking floorboard, and climbed the three steps to hers. If God hadn't taken her yet, maybe she could stay. I tiptoed into the room where the drawn brown curtains fluttered in the icy wind, the windows left open to let her spirit out. There was a lump in the shape of a person under her covers. I pulled the covers down from her face, ready for magnificence like the radiant angels on our Christmas cards, but Mammy's face was contorted and her mouth frozen in a silent scream. Mammy was not an angel; she was a monster.

The next day, she was buried in the cemetery on the top

of the hill, and I wore my best blue dress and black Mary Jane shoes. We put Mammy in the grave on Daddy's family plot, and back in the house, I spent the rest of the day filling people's drinks and making sandwiches for the mourners. They patted my head and said I had to be the woman of the house now Mammy was gone to heaven, but she wasn't in heaven because I witnessed her going into the ground. They were lying, all of them.

For three days they smoked, drank whiskey and ate sandwiches in our house. When I could get away, I lay on her bed, reading her books and inhaling her smell. I brought a bag of books to her grave and read to her. I wrapped her patchwork quilt up tight and put it in a plastic bag to keep her smell on it. Then I put it in another bag and another one and hid it under my bed.

They said I could pray to Mammy in heaven, but I knew she wasn't there. It would be pointless praying to someone dead. Fly high with the angels they said. Lie low with the worms, they meant.

Instead, when I got sad or lonely, I imagined her long auburn hair and her soft belly, swinging me around and laughing. I tried not to think of the face in the bed, which terrorised my dreams.

IT's over four hours later and after eleven when I return to the windowless room, now stinking. Scarlett runs at me, flailing and scratching like a wild animal, and knocks the tray of food out of my hand. The tomato sauce from the pasta splashes, burning my hand, and I push her away from me.

"You locked me in. You left me here on my own." She throws herself on the bed and punches the pillow.

I had to leave her. She needs to understand the power

balance if this is to work. In the time I was gone, she wrecked the room. Books, paper, crayons, paints and toys are strewn everywhere, and the smell is vile.

"We don't disrespect books." I pick up Roald Dahl's *Matilda*, its cover ripped, and replace it on the bookshelf.

"Where did you go?" she manages through her howls.

"I was needed elsewhere. I told you my daddy isn't well. What's that smell?"

She turns away, still bawling, and I see a brown pile in the yellow bucket beside the disco light.

"Is that – poo?"

"I was bursting. You never came back."

I take a deep breath. "You're right. I'm sorry. It's not your fault."

She cries harder, and I let her while I tidy up, then sit on the edge of her bed and rub her leg. She snatches it away and pushes her face into the white wall. Her crying subsides.

"Did you find your swimsuit?" a muffled voice asks.

"Yes, but we need to eat. You must be hungry."

She turns to me, her face blotchy and covered in snot. "But then it will be night-time."

I wink at her. "I don't mind going to the beach in the dark if you don't. It will be an adventure."

There's a flicker in her eyes. "The beach at night-time?"

"Yes, the beach at night-time. Night swimming under the stars. What do you say?"

She bites her lip. "Promise you'll bring me home after."

"Promise."

She gobbles down the food, licking the bowl, and hands it to me. "Let's go."

I check my phone. "Oh no." I slap my forehead, but this time she doesn't laugh. "The beach is closed. What a shame."

She roars again. "But you said..."

"I'll tell you what. Why don't you stay here tonight, and we'll go first thing in the morning? We can have a sleepover."

"I don't want a sleepover. I want to go home now, to my mammy and daddy."

"Your mother knows where you are, silly. You told her you were coming with me to the beach, remember?"

She taps her implants. "My batteries. I need to go home to charge my cochlear batteries."

"Don't you worry." I tap my forehead. "I have that figured out."

"I don't know..."

"It's all great. You told your parents you were coming, and wait until you see the enormous waves at this beach! We'll get ice cream and make sandcastles, and it will be awesome!"

She sniffles. "And after that, you'll bring me home?"

"Of course."

"But the poo is smelly, and I need to do a wee."

"Use the bucket. I'll empty it for you first to get rid of the smell. Don't worry about that at all."

Her eyes grow heavy. "Okay. We can go tomorrow."

13

KAREN

Day 2 – 08:50
Over 15 hours missing

Garda Cormack McCarthy drives us down Dominic Street, Main Street and up Mary Street. Scarlett's painting is folded up and deep in the pocket of my trousers. I don't care that they think this is a stretch; I have to explore every possibility. As we pass through the town, shops open, and another scorching day begins. People step out onto the street from the flats above them, everyone busy with their lives. I want to scream STOP at them all, to scream from the rooftops for help. Our phones beep and ring as we answer call after text after WhatsApp after Facebook message. Old work acquaintances and friends mostly, people whom I haven't heard from in years, and more than a few who led the call for my cancellation.

"Maybe put the phones on silent for now. Take a few minutes to collect your thoughts," Garda McCarthy says.

As we turn the corner, I hear them before I see them. A crowd has gathered outside the three-storey grey building that is Mullingar Garda Station. Helen faces us. "All set?" Her eyes are puffy and bloodshot. I can only imagine what mine are like. It's been over thirteen hours since they arrived at our house. Fifteen hours since reporting Scarlett missing, and there has been no breakthrough, no lead. Except for the picture. If Scarlett wore her implants during the night, her batteries will be dead by now. My breath catches. She must be so scared wherever she is. Why hasn't she come home if she isn't being held captive? Is she injured? In the lake? The woman from the CCTV and the painting flashes in my mind, and I gasp. I have to get the TV appeal and get the word out before my head explodes.

Wear something presentable, they told us. I chose a white shirt, grey cotton trousers and white flats. It felt wrong showering and preparing on precious time, but I didn't know how groomed I should be. I put a dash of mascara and a swipe of red lipstick on and tied my hair into a low ponytail at the nape of my neck. My oversized sunglasses are fake Gucci. Paddy is wearing pinstripe navy trousers from his best suit, a blue business shirt, opened at the collar, and genuine aviator Ray-Bans. Even through the sunglasses he looks shattered. In another lifetime, we could be an anxious couple going to the bank to inquire about a mortgage or a car loan.

The crowd spots us and runs towards the car.

Garda McCarthy switches on his indicator. "I'll pull around the back to be safe."

"Keep your heads down as we go through and ignore them," Helen adds. I try to focus on the back of her seat, but it's difficult with the shouts and taunts at my window.

Murderers.

Where is the child?

Bastards.

Around the back of the station, the Garda car pulls up tight to an open door, and another Garda ushers us down corridors of offices into a small room on the ground floor. Used coffee cups and paper plates are scattered on a table in the centre of the room.

"Take a seat," she says, resting against the windowsill. "My colleague will be along shortly."

We sit in silence for too long before the clickety-click of footsteps hails the arrival of another uniformed Garda, who enters the room, hand outstretched.

"Superintendent Aidan Fogarty, Garda Press Office. Sorry for the dreadful circumstances in which we meet." The tall, groomed man shakes our hands firmly.

Paddy sits up straight and puts his arm around the back of my chair. "Paddy O'Hara and this is my wife, Karen."

Superintendent Fogarty remains standing and removes two A4 sheets from the document folder he carries, handing one to Paddy. "This is the script we prepared for you. Have a read through it, and let me know if you have any questions." He tilts his head at me. "How are you bearing up?"

My eyes fill up, and I shake my head.

"We're not," Paddy says. "It's a nightmare."

I try to focus on my script, scanning the words, all too familiar. How many times have I heard these words on TV when someone goes missing? Words that stopped me briefly, considering how awful it must be for the parents, before going on with my day, preparing dinner or helping with homework. *Or other things.*

"Can we veer from the script?" Paddy asks.

"It's best to stick to the script first, and after the formal appeal, there will be time for you to say your own piece. Then, by all means, say what you want."

As we read through the printed words, there is a low hum of voices outside the room.

"The conference room has been set up for the appeal. It's busy and can be intimidating walking in there, but it will let us get the word out; the more people who know, the quicker we will find Scarlett. I'll go in first, followed by you, Paddy, then Karen. I will manage the running order and call on you to speak when it is your time."

"How long will the appeal be?" Paddy asks.

"No more than ten minutes. If there're questions you don't feel comfortable answering, pass them to me. I'm well versed in this process."

"What kind of questions?" I ask.

"Ah, sometimes the story gets ahead of itself. Questions can become loaded. Don't worry, we'll cross that bridge if we come to it."

I take Scarlett's painting from the zoo from my trousers pocket, unfold it and pass it to him. "My daughter painted this picture of someone she says she's been playing with. Notice how she is blonde with a green top and blue trousers. We checked the CCTV of the zoo, and there was a woman matching her description there. I'm going to show this picture."

He studies the picture. "I wouldn't recommend it. If required, we'll use a still from the zoo." He hands the picture back to me as the door opens, and the chatter grows loud.

"But Scarlett drew this, and the same woman was on the CCTV. She has—"

"Ready for you now," another Garda calls in the door.

Fogarty takes the chair opposite us, pushing away a paper plate and looking me straight in the eye. "Karen, we want to get Scarlett home, and the best way to do that is to follow my direction. Can you trust my experience?"

I nod. Paddy takes my hand, and I let him lead me into the adjacent conference room, diverting my gaze from the packed room. We take our places at the top of the room behind a long desk on which journalists scatter microphones. There's a hush.

The appeal goes by in a blur until it is my turn to speak. I read from the script I hold in my trembling hand.

"My name is Karen O'Hara." My voice cracks.

Paddy squeezes my hand. "You can do this."

I clear my throat. "Yesterday evening between 5:30pm and 6:45pm, our daughter, Scarlett O'Hara, went missing from our home on the shore of Lough Owel, outside Mullingar on the main Dublin to Longford Road. She's eight years old, approximately four feet in height, has brown, long curly hair and blue eyes. She's profoundly deaf with two cochlear implants and can hear nothing without them. We need to get her home before her batteries die, which will be in the next few hours." I break down. "I'm sorry—"

Fogarty reads the remainder of my script, including the emergency contact details. My head is spinning, but I focus on my breathing until the appeal is opened to the floor.

A reporter stands up. "Joan Rafferty, the *Irish Journal*. Question for Karen."

I search the crowd and locate the reporter, a tall woman with short brown hair.

"Karen, I believe CCTV footage shows you leaving your house with Scarlett on Thursday morning and then returning that night without her. Is it true nobody has seen her since then?"

"That is not true. She was in our home until at least half past five yesterday."

Hands fly into the air as Garda Fogarty selects one.

"Kevin Roche, *Independent Thinking*. Karen?"

Paddy releases my hand, joining both of his on the table in front of him. I nod at the journalist to continue.

"The last time Scarlett was seen was Thursday morning. Is it true you told your husband not to check on her on Thursday night, and he didn't see her on Friday morning?"

"It is not true, no. Paddy said goodbye to Scarlett

yesterday before he went to work, and there's footage of her in Dublin Zoo on Thursday."

"But Paddy didn't see her on Friday morning."

"He did see her, he said goodbye, but she was asleep." My hand goes to my right pocket in my trousers, and I finger the picture.

Garda Fogarty leans into his microphone. "One more question, folks."

"Heather Farrell, *Irish Voice*. Question for Karen."

Paddy exhales and clasps his hands behind his head.

"In an interview on *Good Morning, Ireland* last year, Karen, you admitted you didn't want your daughter, Scarlett. In light of current circumstances, do you regret saying that?"

I narrow my eyes at the tall journalist with cropped blonde hair, and she blushes. "What do you think? Of course I regret saying that; I regret it every day. I was trying to illustrate how bad a place I was in to help others who were struggling. It was a bad choice of words, and I have paid dearly for that. I love my daughter. I would never hurt her intentionally."

I wince. I've said the wrong words again. *Intentionally.* I know I'm not supposed to, but when the muttering in the room rises, I take the picture out and hold it up. "This is a picture Scarlett painted on Thursday evening, and I believe this woman has her. Scarlett calls her Hope, the same name as her dead sister, but I believe she's a woman who has been grooming Scarlett. If you recognise her, please contact the Gardai."

The room falls silent as journalists stare back at me open-mouthed.

"Are you out of your fucking mind?" Paddy spits under his breath as someone in the room titters.

Fogarty leans into his microphone. "This is a stressful time for the family, as I am sure you will understand." He rises to his feet. "That is all for the minute, folks. As stated, we are grateful for any assistance in locating Scarlett O'Hara. Anyone in the area of Lough Owel and the N4 between the hours of 4pm and 8pm on Friday evening who may have seen anything unusual, or anyone with information, please come forward. CCTV, dashcam footage, anything that can help. Check those outhouses and land, and keep vigilant for her on surrounding roads. All developments will be relayed as they happen. Thank you for your time."

We follow Fogarty out of the room, cameras flashing, and return to the meeting room. He closes the door behind us.

"Why did you undermine me?" I hiss to Fogarty. "That woman has my daughter."

Paddy stands between me and Fogarty, his face millimetres from mine. "You showed them a painting by an eight-year-old even though you were advised not to. What were you thinking?"

"It's a clear picture."

"It's a fucking stick picture. You looked like a nutter!"

"Calm down, folks; everyone is under pressure. Take a beat." Fogarty holds his hands up. "Karen, the direction we give is for a good reason. We know how these things play out. However, what's done is done, and we got the word out, which was our intention."

Helen opens the door. "DI McGovern, the detective heading up this case, wants to have a quick word before I bring you home."

We leave the station in the back of the marked police car; the crowd outside larger in anger and size than when we arrived. We drive past them and out of town and onto the N4 in silence, the air conditioning a small mercy from the July heat.

"If someone wanted money, would they have been in contact by now?" Paddy asks.

"Not necessarily," Garda Cormack McCarthy says. "We're monitoring your emails and your landline. If someone makes contact with you directly, as already stated, it is vital you let us know."

Before we left the station, the detective in charge told us not to facilitate personal contact with blackmailers. Detective Inspector Dave McGovern, a man about our age with brown hair and glasses, ran us through things we should not do, including taking ransom or blackmail demands into our own hands.

"Of course," Paddy replies. "But if it's money they want, we'll pay it. Goes without saying."

"Can you find more CCTV of the blonde woman in the zoo? There might be a clearer picture of her at the entrance or exit, and check the other places we went to. If we see her face—"

"Would you stop it?" Paddy's voice is tired. "She was one of many women in a busy playground on a summer's day. One of many people who spoke to Scarlett and other children."

"A blonde woman whose clothes matched those in Scarlett's picture with no children? That's highly coincidental."

"That's exactly what it is. A coincidence."

"Do you have a pen?" I ask Helen, ignoring him. She passes a blue biro back to me. On the back of Scarlett's picture, I write.

Mullingar Town Park Monday 3–5pm

Molly's Pet Farm Tuesday 11am until 4pm

I hand it back to her. "You already have the places we visited over the last few weeks, but these are the most recent places we went that Scarlett drew Hope after. Please check them out, maybe they have CCTV, and if the colours in the clothes on the footage matches the colours Hope used that day, then surely there's something in that."

"I don't know—"

"If I'm wrong, at least we can eliminate my theory. But what if I'm right? What if the same woman is in all of these places? That's not a coincidence."

Helen looks to Garda McCarthy.

I continue, "She's been out all night; we have to try something. For God's sake, you're a mother, Helen. Have some empathy. I'm losing my mind here."

I lie back against the seat and close my eyes, tears of frustration and exhaustion flowing. What I would give to be back pushing Scarlett on the swings again, and it hurts to think how absent I was at our last trip to the park. I was feet away from her but absorbed in my phone. My phone. I unmute it, and it rings with an unknown number. I answer.

"Hello. Karen speaking."

Helen extends her hand for my phone, but I hold it tight.

"Um." It's a woman. "Is this Karen O'Hara?"

"Yes, speaking."

"Um... I think I might have seen your little girl."

I jolt upright. "Where? Where is she?"

"I don't know for sure, but a little girl and a woman arrived late yesterday to the disused cottage at the top of our hill. The girl had brown curly hair, and the woman was blonde, just like in Scarlett's picture you showed on TV. I don't know. It might be nothing, but I thought I should call."

"You did the right thing. Thank you so, so, so, so much. Where do you live?"

"Rathowen, not far from you off the Longford Road. I can WhatsApp the Eircode to you."

"What is it?" Helen whispers, and I hold up a finger to request a minute.

"Please do that," I say to the woman on the phone. "Can you send it straight away?"

"Coming through now."

I end the call. "Go straight to Rathowen. That was a woman who thinks Scarlett might be there with a blonde woman. They arrived last night to a disused cottage." My phone pings as the Eircode comes through.

Helen relays the details to her colleagues through her radio. "We'll check it out right after we drop you folks—"

"No way," Paddy says. "We're going with you."

"Your call," Garda McCarthy tells Helen, keeping his eyes on the road.

"You can come with us," Helen says, "but you must follow our directions."

"We will," I say.

"And manage your expectations. This is a lead, that's all. There may be many, many more. People mean well, but ninety-nine per cent of the calls we'll get won't lead to anything."

"It's the best we've had so far," Paddy says.

14

ELAINE

Day 2 – 09:00

I carry a tray with breakfast down to Scarlett, down to the room Daddy converted for me. After Mammy died, he stayed on the farm from sunrise to sunset and drank whiskey every night. He'd call me down from bed and rant. "You killed your mother."

"I didn't, Daddy," I'd object. "I loved her."

"Ye did. Killed her stone dead. Getting pupped with you triggered her cancer, and you didn't even have the effing decency to be a boy. At least then you'd have been some use on the farm instead of the waste of space that ye are."

Other nights he'd sit me on his lap and hold me close, his whiskey breath on my neck. "I'm so lonely, Elaine."

"You can get married again," I'd suggest.

"No woman will want me with you hanging around. I never wanted you, but your mother wouldn't listen. You've ruined my life."

Most nights he'd pass out in Mammy's chair, but sometimes his eyes would darken, and he'd turn violent. Those nights I took Mammy's quilt and slept on her grave. On the rare occasion I stayed home for fear of freezing, he'd pull me from the bed, take his shotgun from the gun safe and march me to this very room in my bare feet and nightie.

"I should shoot you right now," he'd say as I trembled and begged down the barrel of his gun. "Do the world a favour, you worthless piece of shit."

When he put a bed in this room, in my innocence, I thought it was a kindness. It wasn't, it was unimaginably grotesque. Then came the one-way lock on the door – anyone could walk in, but you could only leave with the key. Nobody would listen when I told them; no one would hear a bad word about Tom Murtagh, the poor widowed farmer, salt of the earth, a gentleman. I blanked out most of those years, and at age fifteen, I packed a holdall and took the bus to Dublin. I never planned to return to Ballygrave, but life is full of surprises. This time, however, I'm in charge.

"Wakey, wakey, rise and shine." I carry a tray containing a bowl of porridge with honey and a glass of orange juice, Scarlett's favourite breakfast. She is fast asleep, her implants on the locker beside her bed. Her tousled brown curls hang over her tender face, and Mammy's quilt rises and falls with her breath. Such a beautiful child.

I sit on the edge of the bed, and she bounces like a coiled spring, like the feral cats in the yard, on high alert. I show her the breakfast I've prepared for her.

She peers into the bowl and pulls a face. "What's that?"

"Porridge and honey, your favourite."

She rubs her eyes and reaches for her implants. She switches them on and puts them on her ears, fixing the disks to her head. She looks into the bowl again and gags.

Scarlett loves porridge. It's all about giving them choices and exposing them to a wide variety of healthy foods. I must admit to being naughty and adding organic honey to sweeten it, but it's better than the boxed sugary processed cereals in our shops. Children will eat healthy when given healthy.

Karen is turning out to be quite the liar. What else will I discover? First the art, then the porridge. Yesterday's art, scattered around the room, revealed Scarlett is no Michelangelo. She might love drawing, and I know she's a kid, but she's average at best.

"I thought porridge was your favourite. Let me see what else I have."

She grabs my arm, her eyes wide. "No, I'll eat it. Please don't leave me on my own again."

She spoons the porridge into her tiny mouth, suppressing gags. I hold the bowl under her chin. "Spit it out. Let me make you something else."

She releases a masticated blob into the bowl and pants.

"What would you like for breakfast?"

"Breakfast? Is it morning?" She jumps out of the bed. "Come on, let's go to the beach."

"Eat something, and then we can go. What would you like?"

She glances upwards. "I don't know what you have. I'll come with you and see."

"Oh, I'd love to show you, but you might get sick if you come too close to my daddy. How about a bowl of Sugar Pops?"

"I want to go."

"After breakfast."

She closes her eyes and nods. I bring the porridge upstairs, where Daddy is awake. I switch on the TV and take my place in the chair beside his bed, spooning in the regurgitated mess. The news comes on, and I increase the volume when I see who is on it.

"Well, well, Daddy. If it isn't our good friend Karen."

"We need to get her home before her batteries die..."

I laugh. "Not so sure of herself now, eh? I wonder what she'd say if she knew her daughter who she never wanted was here."

He groans.

"In our special room!"

Daddy refuses the rest of the porridge, so I give him his medication and a quick rubdown. It's been two days since his last one, but already his muscles are weaker. When I return to the basement with the coloured cereal, Scarlett is sitting at her desk, drawing two girls holding hands. I lay the bowl beside her. "That's a lovely picture. Is it me and you?"

She bites her lip. "No, me and Mammy. I don't want to go to the beach anymore. I want to go home."

I sit on her bed. "Don't be silly, we agreed. First the beach and then I'll bring you home. We'll have a lovely day, like we planned."

She looks me straight in the eye. "No, I want to go home. Bring me home."

"You're mean," I whimper, exaggerating a frown. "I let you sleep in my house and brought you breakfast, and I want to go to the beach, but you don't care about me." I put my head in my hands and pretend to cry. "And my daddy is sick, and I thought you were my friend."

I wait and wait until a little hand pats my back. "I'll go for a little while. But I'll need to charge my batteries."

"Scarlett, I love you. You're my best friend."

She stands. "Let's go."

"Almost ready to go. I'll get some batteries and put the picnic together first."

"No, no, no." She starts to cry again. "Don't leave me in this room. Let me go home."

I push her away and pull the door behind me, but her screaming is still audible. I swap the clothes from the washing machine to the dryer, reload the washing machine and switch both on full cycles to drown out the noise. I don't want to take any chances. She'll get used to being here. It's normal for a child to experience separation anxiety, but after an adjustment period and acceptance, they settle eventually. I climb the stairs, thinking about her face when she sees my great surprise, but when I enter the hallway, I feel someone watching me. I turn to see a man at the front door.

"Hello, ma'am?" He peers in through the glass panel.

I hold my breath and stand still.

"Ma'am, I can see you. It's the police."

The door is stiff and jammed, with junk mail backed up on the old carpet. We never use this door. I yank hard and stumble backwards when it gives, falling to the floor. An over-weight Garda holds my hands up, but he helps me to my feet in a lather of sweat.

"Sorry for disturbing you. Garda Waters, I'm in the area looking for a child. You may have heard she's missing." He hands me a flyer.

Scarlett O'Hara
8 years old.
Last seen near Lough Owel, Westmeath, 5:30pm, Friday 23rd July.
Any information contact Mullingar Garda station

A photo of her completes the page. "She's beautiful," I say, focusing on the flyer and trying to think at lightning speed. Over his shoulder I see a marked car in the front yard. It looks empty, which means this could be a routine door-to-door call. Otherwise, wouldn't there be two Gardai? Hell, there'd be a lot more than two. But what if they're planning to ambush me? Is this a trick?

"It's shocking." I fix my hair. "The poor family. I heard about her on the news. I'm praying she'll turn up."

"She hasn't yet, unfortunately, but we're doing everything

we can. If you see or hear anything, can you contact us on the number there?"

"Of course I will. Anything to help, Garda." He turns to leave, and I'm about to close the front door when a wail comes from upstairs. He stops.

"My father," I explain, maintaining my composure. "He's terminally ill. I'm his carer."

Daddy cries out again.

"Would you mind if I come back in for a minute?" he asks, and I do mind but welcome him into the front room. He fills Mammy's old brown armchair, and I sit opposite him on the floral sofa. We haven't changed this room since she died. As if, if we don't move the stuff, she will be still here. Books fill the dressers, and there is an inch of dust on the fireplace. China ornaments dot the room, and there is a reminder of her cigarettes in the yellowed lace curtains and the brown velvet drapes. Dust dances in the sunbeams, and the Garda sneezes as another wail comes from upstairs.

"My father is terminally ill."

"What's the matter with him?" He produces a white handkerchief from his trouser pocket and wipes his streaming eyes.

"I hope that's not contagious."

He sneezes again. "No. Just allergies."

"Daddy had a brain haemorrhage. Then he got a diagnosis of cancer. They tried to treat it, but it was too advanced. I came home to mind him."

"That's shocking kind of you."

I shrug. "You do for family."

The washing machine starts its spin cycle in the background.

"Would you like to go see him?" I ask, pre-empting him. This is inconvenient but so far manageable, and maybe satisfying this Garda will be enough to keep others away.

"Yes, that would be great, thank you."

I lead him up the old carpeted stairs that creak as he climbs, him dragging on the rail. On the dark landing at the top of the stairs, I walk up three more stairs and knock on the heavy wooden door.

"Daddy, you have a guest." I show the Garda into his bedroom. Daddy's eyes widen as we approach. The smell is more pungent than usual, as if the whole house is trying to eject our visitor.

Garda Waters leans to me. "What's his name?" His breath smells of bacon and coffee.

"Tom Murtagh, isn't that your name, Daddy? The best dairy farmer in all of North Westmeath."

Today on Loose Lips, *we will speak to author and playwright Henry Holmes, and on day two in the case of the disappearance of Scarlett O'Hara we ask, do we overshare on social media?*

Daddy moans, and I change the channel. "He gets agitated. The doctors say there's not much going on in there, but I don't know. Sad stories like this affect him. Now, Daddy, that's better. A bit of Jonathan and Jennifer."

The Garda breaks into a fit of coughing.

"I think you need to leave, it sounds like you may be coming down with something, and my father is vulnerable."

"Yes, of course. I'll be off, Tom, but don't worry, I've nothing contagious. It's just allergies." He leaves the room, wiping his forehead.

I wink at Daddy, who closes his eyes, then go to the gasping man on the landing. He wheezes, holding the banister with one hand and my arm with the other. "I need some air."

I hold my nerve and sigh. "No problem at all. I don't want him to get more ill, you know? It's hard enough to see him suffer like this. It would kill me if he picked something up. He'd never survive it."

"I understand." He tests the strength of the stairs as he descends, and I open the front door, an easier task this time. He sneezes again as he spills out the front door. "Thanks for your time, ma'am, I appreciate it. Don't hesitate to contact us if you see anything at all."

"I won't. Mind yourself." He lowers himself into his car and drives out the front gates as the spin cycle finishes, and the house is quiet again except for the faint screaming.

Daddy won't open his eyes as I enter his room.

"Did you think that was clever? Did you think he would understand you? You decrepit old, useless, lie-in-bed fool?"

His eyes are still closed, so I round the bed, lean over his face and shake him. "Open your eyes. Listen to me."

His eyes fly open.

"After all I do for you. Giving up my home, my work, to come and mind you here, and this is how you repay me?"

Daddy's face was a picture when I walked back into his bedroom last year. The room was hot and stuffy, the house unchanged since I left over twenty years previously.

"Hello, Daddy. Good to be back."

"A stroke," the doctor said. "He doesn't have any movement, and we don't know how much damage there was."

I leaned down and whispered to Daddy, "You evil bastard, it's time for payback."

He cried out, trembling. How the tables had turned.

"Ah now, Daddy. No need to thank me."

The doctor put his hand on his shoulder. "Tom, it's your daughter, Elaine. Back to see you. Isn't she great, altogether?"

"Don't worry, Doctor," I said and winked at Daddy. "I'll take good care of him."

And that's what I had done, not because he deserves it, but because I'm a good person. He'll die soon, and God forgive me, but I hope he burns in hell for all eternity.

15

KAREN

Day 2 – 10:00

Rathowen is a small town halfway between Mullingar and Longford on the main road from Dublin to the west of Ireland. The sun beats through the window as we slow to a halt behind a long line of cars held up by a tractor ahead. Garda Cormack McCarthy puts the siren on, and the traffic parts for us. He speeds out, and cars make way as we speed up the other side of the road.

"Do you know anyone she could be with in Rathowen? A friend or family member?" Helen holds the handle above her door as we swerve and I take Paddy's weight.

"Not that I can think of," I reply as the car turns off the N4 and onto a tree-lined road. We pass intermittent bungalows and farmhouses until we reach two patrol cars blocking the road at the foot of a hill. Garda McCarthy parks the car on the grass verge to the left, and another male Garda approaches. Helen rolls down the window, the hot air gushing in.

"As far as here for these folks." The Garda folds his arms and doesn't make eye contact with us.

"No way, I'm her father. I want to go with you."

The police officer remains firm. "This is as far as you can come, sir."

There is a grey two-storey house on the hill, and a group of women with folded arms gather across from us on the narrow road. The Gardai communicate on radios at the foot of the hill. I approach the huddle of women, and a woman in her thirties steps forward.

"You're Karen, right? It was me who called you. See that house up there on the hill? There hasn't been anyone in it for years, but yesterday evening, a woman and child arrived, and I thought that was strange even then, but when I saw your appeal on TV this morning, I had to call you. I told all this to the guards too, but I found your number online, and well, it was because of the picture you showed that I made the connection. The child had brown hair, and the woman was a blonde. Anyway, I thought you might like to speak to me yourself, see what I saw. I know I would if it were my child."

"I heard her. This morning," another woman says. "I was bringing the dog for a walk through the woods when I was sure I heard a child crying at the back of the house."

"What was she wearing?" I ask, although that is now a moot question. Whoever has her will have changed her clothes. This makes my stomach drop.

"I didn't see her. When I got closer, the crying stopped. I didn't pay much heed, but in hindsight, I should have. Mary heard her too."

"She was skipping, but I didn't see what she was wearing," another woman says.

"What did you say?"

"I never looked. I didn't realise—"

"No, the piece before that. What did you say she was doing?"

"Skipping."

"With a rope? Rope-skipping?"

"Yes. I think so. What? Why?"

Black blotches appear in my vision, and my head goes light. The woman takes a step back. "Oh, love, what's wrong? Garda, help! Garda!"

My mouth is flapping, but I can't speak. I can't catch my breath. Paddy runs to me. "What's going on? What happened?"

I vomit on the road, splattering the women, who back away. "It's not her," I manage when I catch a breath. "It's not Scarlett up there."

"How do you know?"

"Scarlett can't skip."

"Of course she can skip. She's a child."

I don't have the energy to mince my words. "Paddy, why do you think I bring her to occupational therapy every week? Her balance is shot from her deafness."

The police radio calls out for Helen, and she walks away. The speaker's voice is loud, and I hang on every word.

"Identities checked and validated... This is a mother and child, not the child Scarlett O'Hara... All documentation checks out... Not our woman."

Helen can barely make eye contact as she returns to us. "It's not Scarlett."

"I can't take anymore," I wail, and Paddy holds me.

"We'll keep looking," she says. "I promise you that. We'll do everything in our power to get her home to you. Come on, I'll take you home."

A DIFFERENT GARDA waves us through the makeshift orange barrier at the top of our lane and outside our house. Helen guides us through the gathered crowd, but that journalist from the *Irish Times* runs towards us with a microphone, flanked by a cameraman. "Karen, a word?"

Garda McCarthy steps between her and us. "Not now, Heather."

Once inside, the house seems empty, all the people gone from earlier. We sit silently in the living area – Paddy, me and the two Gardai – when an elderly lady in a skirted suit comes from the kitchen, making me jump. "Jesus, my heart!"

"Sorry, didn't mean to startle you. Karen, your mother has been calling the landline," she tells me, like she has a right to be in our house. "I'm Vera, by the way, the fort-holder."

I raise an eyebrow at Helen. "You're in safe hands with Vera," she says. "She's with victim support. Let her look after you, maybe arrange some food while you get your heads down. She's an angel."

I agree to coffee, which Vera decides she will fetch, along with sandwiches from town, to give Paddy and me space.

Helen yawns. "We'll head off for a few hours. Some sleep, some food, and hopefully by tonight there will be no need for us to return to you folks. Our colleagues are working hard, and they'll keep you updated. Call for anything you need; there're cars outside."

I drag myself upstairs when they leave, trying to divert my gaze away from Scarlett's room as I pass, but the pink butterflies on her wall flutter in the gentle breeze, and I am in her room. I sit on her bed and inhale her baby-bath scent. Where the hell is she? I close my eyes and am awoken by a noise – a tractor or is it a helicopter? Who opened the windows? Was that me? When were they last closed? I call my mother, who answers in a fit of coughing.

"Mam?"

"Karen, darling, where have you been?" Her voice is gentle. "I've been trying to reach you."

"I must have been out of range, Mam. We did the TV appeal, then somebody thought they saw Scarlett, so we went to the house, but it was a false alarm."

"Oh, darling. This is awful. I should be there with you."

It's not often I ask my mother to go the extra mile for me, and I'm irked I have to, but I'm beyond pride. "I need you, Mam. Please come home."

"There are no free flights until Monday, darling." She inhales with a wheeze and breaks into another bout of chesty coughing. "Listen to me, Karen, us Sullivans are made of stern stuff. It's time to pull on that. Until I get there, I will be with you every step of the way in spirit." She coughs again. "We'll find her."

"Are you okay, Mam? You don't sound so good."

"I am. I will be. Something and nothing. Oh." she coughs again. "Before I go, is the weasel there?"

"Paddy?"

"Who else?"

"Um, yes, he's in the garden, I think."

"Put him on."

I descend the stairs in my bare feet, and through the kitchen window I see Paddy in the garden, talking on his phone. He paces, deep in conversation. I watch for a few minutes until he sees me at the window and ends the call.

"It's my mother. She wants to talk to you."

He takes the phone from me, his face flushed. "Hello, Felicia. Yes. Yes. Of course." He continues the call down the garden before returning with my phone.

"I'm back, Mam."

"In case you're wondering what I said, I told him I'll be there as soon as I can, but in the meantime to watch out for you and call me with any news. I do love you, darling."

"Love you too, Mam." That was weird. We never said that to each other before.

In the kitchen, the counter is gleaming, and the smell of lemon and bleach is strong. I would put the kettle on, but Vera is bringing coffee. I'm floating with fatigue, but I know I won't sleep.

Paddy comes inside. "Karen, I'm worried."

"Me too. I'm going to have a shower, then get back out after we eat." I should hug him, but I head for the stairs.

He blocks my passage. "Did something happen that you haven't told me?"

I push by him, deciding against the shower. Upstairs, I grab my runners.

He's hot on my heels. "Did it? You would tell me, wouldn't you?"

I lace up my runners, my blood pressure rising. "Have a chat with yourself, Paddy."

From the landing he calls after me, "When did you stop taking your medication?" I stop, halfway down, and turn to see him holding papers. My unfilled prescriptions. "You didn't pick them up this month. Or last."

"Where did you get them?"

"In your purse. You've been acting strange. I didn't want to believe—"

"How dare you go into my purse?" I hate how defensive I sound.

"Why did you stop taking your meds?" His face softens, but my heart is thumping, and I'm ashamed. I don't want to have this conversation.

"None of your business."

"Karen, tell me!"

"A while ago."

"When?"

"A few months."

He puts his face in his hands. "Why didn't you tell me? You said we'd talk about your anxiety after the last time."

"My anxiety was fine. Is fine. But I was like a zombie on those new drugs. Zoned out, sleeping, whacked out. You must have noticed."

"Oh, Karen." He shakes his head. "You swore you would talk to me about decisions like this. You said you wouldn't bottle up your problems ever again."

"How can I talk to you about my problem when" – I know it's unfair to continue, but I spit the words regardless – "you're the reason I have problems."

He gasps as the doorbell rings. I descend the remaining steps and open the door, expecting to find that woman, Vera, carrying supplies, but instead two Gardai stand at the door. I recognise the man as the detective in charge of the case who spoke to us before we left the station, but the young blonde woman with plaits is unfamiliar.

"DI Samantha Clarke and this is my colleague DI McGovern. Karen, can you come down to the station? We'd like to have a wee chat," she says.

I turn to Paddy for an explanation.

"I had no choice. I had to tell them about your episode."

16

KAREN

Seven years ago

"It's not unusual to feel this way, especially after the compounded trauma you've experienced from your accident, losing a child, and Scarlett's recent diagnosis of profound hearing loss. Please don't overly worry, these things usually settle themselves, but if things don't improve, come back, and I'll give you something to help you through this."

Dr Holmes of the City medical practice walks me and my baby out of his consultation room, through the busy waiting area to reception, where I pay €50 for the privilege of being told I'm normal. Maybe I wasn't honest with him about how bad things are. Maybe I didn't mention I'm filled with anger and grief, that I'm wiped out, exhausted, lonely and now frustrated he didn't look closer to see it himself. I wanted the doctor to say I needed help. I wanted him to give me pills, but all he gives me is a business card.

Brigid Carpenter – Grief and postpartum counselling.

There is hope.

"She's very good," he says.

Outside the surgery, I place my soft pink bundle into her pram and tuck the padded blankets in under her. It's a dark and cold January morning, and she's asleep, which means she'll be awake when we get home and for the rest of the long, long day. I zip up my black padded coat, pop in my earphones and set off for my daily morning walk. It's not even 8am, and the day stretches out in front of me like an endless void. It's hard to fill days. I never thought about it before, being busy with school and then work, but it is. There's only so much stimulation a five-month-old baby can provide although they can go days without sleep. I've found a newsagent with a friendly assistant, and even though it's a good walk away, I go regularly for the chat, making myself pass by some days to keep a scrap of dignity. I've been awake since 4am when I gave up the hope of more shut-eye and got out of bed. *Hope.*

I wheel her pram past office blocks, lights switching on like Christmas, and observe young hipsters opening coffee shops. The Irish Financial Services Centre, or IFSC, is in the heart of Dublin city, just north of the River Liffey, and attracts high-flyers from around the country. People going places like I was.

The aroma of coffee floats on the winter air, sipped from reusable mugs by people with a purpose. Well-turned-out commuters dashing to high-rise offices in suits, carrying expensive bags. A woman in a sharp trouser suit and court shoes crosses my path, almost tripping over the pram, but she doesn't acknowledge me and continues on. I don't judge her; she's me in another lifetime. The one where I didn't get pregnant, where Paddy didn't get my promotion and where I wasn't wishing the day was over when it had only begun. Hard to believe it was me who hired him in the first place.

No point in thinking about that. Instead, I tune in to the soothing kindness of the morning talk show host on the radio and walk. And walk.

This morning, as Scarlett screamed in my arms, Paddy told me to go to the doctor, that he was worried about me but that he had an important meeting and couldn't come with me. His words were like a twisting dagger to my heart. I was his team lead, and I was good at my job. It should have been me in that meeting. The pregnancy was a shock, but nothing compared to the sickness. Morning to night, I could barely lift my head off the pillow. Paddy got the promotion, and I had yet to return to work.

The fresh air and movement of two laps of the city centre releases enough endorphins to make most days bearable, but I finish my third lap, and they have yet to kick in. Scarlett still sleeps, so I go again. Up Talbot Street, North Earle Street and left onto O'Connell Street. Paddy would look after her to let me get some sleep when he comes home from work, but I don't want him to.

If he hadn't answered his phone while driving, Hope would be here, and Scarlett wouldn't be deaf. The thought makes me so mad I gulp, swallowing air and coughing. I take a bottle of water from the tray under the pram when I'm aware of where I stand. O'Connell Bridge. A sharp wind rises off the Liffey, its dark navy water high. The grey foam on the choppy waves should be menacing, but it's not. Closing my eyes, I imagine the waves of the sea lapping up on the shores of a beach somewhere exotic like Ibiza or Crete, where we had our honeymoon.

The whiff of a soiled nappy pulls me out of my daydream. I peep into the pram to find Scarlett awake and glaring up at me. I lift her out, and she fusses.

I hold her tight and stare down at the deep water. Her pink pram suit cocoons her, and she presses her soft face against mine. Her cheek is burning from teething or a fever; either way it's going to be another tough day and night. Her chubby fingers explore the inside of my mouth as the water splashes against the Liffey walls, mesmerising me, enticing me in. To throw my legs over...

Stop it.

... and submit to the waves. It would all be over. No more pain. A driver beeps from a passing bus, jolting me from my trance and back to reality. I run with Scarlett, leaving the pram on the bridge, and call Paddy. As if she can sense it, Scarlett breaks into high-pitched screaming and tries to wriggle out of my arms.

"I need help," I cry down the phone over her screams. "Paddy, help me. I'm going crazy."

"One moment," he says in a calm voice, then after a few seconds, "Karen, you know I have this meeting this morning. What's going on?"

People stare at me as they walk by, I'm sobbing uncontrollably, and Scarlett is howling at the top of her lungs and wriggling in my arms. I run into an alley and slide down a wall onto the ground.

"You need to come and get us. I'm not well, Paddy, and I'm scared."

"Where are you?"

"O'Connell Street."

"Paddy, are you joining us?" a man calls on his end of the phone.

"Two minutes," Paddy replies, then whispers, "Could you make your way to the office? It's only around the corner."

"No, I can't, Paddy. I almost jumped into the Liffey with Scarlett, and I'm scared I'm going to do something stupid. You need to come for us right fucking now!"

17

Day 2 – 14:00

"We're not going to the beach, are we?" Scarlett asks. She's calm now and lying on her bed, tracing her finger on the wall.

I scrub the wall, attempting to remove her crayon scribbles from the walls. She destroyed the room after I left.

"Why did you bring me here?"

"I brought you some clean clothes, sweetie." I change the subject and give her my favourite dress from when I was her age. A blue tissue paper cotton dress that swings from the chest when twirled. I found it in my wardrobe when I came home.

She removes her passata-splattered T-shirt and lets the dress fall over her head. My breath catches.

"I mean why take me?" she asks.

I put the sponge down and sit on her bed, beside her. "Because you are wonderful. You deserve all the love in the world."

She scrunches her nose. "You're mean."

It's hard to explain to an adult let alone a child. I try to phrase it in another way, one she'll understand.

"Do you know sometimes bad things happen?"

"Like you taking me?"

"No. Not like that. When I was little, my mammy died."

"How?"

"From cancer. She was sick before she had me, but she got better. Then, when I was eight, she got sick again."

I lie beside her, and she doesn't react.

"The cancer my mammy had was called ovarian cancer. It meant she couldn't have any more children after me. My daddy was angry that I was a girl because he wanted a boy to give the farm to. His daddy left the farm to him, and his daddy left it to his daddy before that. He had no sons to leave his farm to, and he was lonely. He blamed me for everything, including killing my mammy."

"Can girls be farmers?"

I laugh. "Girls can do anything. My daddy is very old-fashioned. He didn't think girls should do that kind of work and did it all himself until he got sick. He thought girls should be in the kitchen, not on the farm."

She twirls a curl around her index finger. "If you give him medicine, will he get better?"

I smile. "You are very sweet, but I don't think so. He's very old."

She sits up, a huge smile on her face. "I know. You could have a baby, and it could be a boy, and he could work on the farm, and I could go home to my mammy and daddy, and we'd all live happily ever after."

The innocence.

"Honey, I did have a little girl, a long time ago, but she was needed in heaven."

She tilts her head. "What was her name?"

I swallow the lump in my throat. "Emily."

Her eyes widen. "Did your baby die?"

"She did. She was so lovely, my Emily." I brush a curl from her face. "I think she would have looked just like you."

"Can you make another baby?"

"I would love nothing more than to have this house full of laughter, but the cancer that got my mammy is genetic."

"Genetic?"

"It means I got it too."

Her lip wobbles. "Are you going to die?"

I rub her head. "No, they caught it early, but they had to take my womb and ovaries, and that means I won't get to be a mammy ever again."

She wipes the tear falling from my face. "That's sad."

"Terribly sad. What do you want to be when you grow up?"

"A YouTuber."

I burst out laughing. "That's a new one on me. Well, all I ever wanted was to be a mammy. When other children in my class wanted to be actors and astronauts and pilots, I wanted to be a mother. I missed my lovely mammy every minute of every day, and when she died, nobody loved me."

"My mammy is lovely too. She loves me like you loved Emily. I should go home."

I don't think so.

"Not loved. Love. I love Emily and always will. Not like your mother." I go back to scrubbing the walls.

She starts to cry again. "My mammy loves me."

"She doesn't love you. She doesn't keep you safe like you deserve and need. I can't allow you to go back to that."

She growls, raising the bedside lamp over her head, her face contorted in rage.

"Honey." I don't raise my voice. "I would think twice before throwing that."

She pauses before slamming the lamp back down on the locker.

"Good girl."

She puts her head into her hands and sobs. "I hate you."

I scrub the wall, the writing coming off with the soapy water. "That's okay. I'll love you anyway. Like my mammy loved me."

"I want to go home to my mammy; she loves me."

"I don't think someone who wishes you were dead loves you."

She shakes her head. "She doesn't."

"She does; she even said it on telly. Here, I'll show you."

As she watches the clip from *Good Morning, Ireland* I downloaded to my phone this morning, her world crumbles with every word from Karen's mouth.

"I never wanted to be a mother... never planned for a child... She was diagnosed as deaf as a baby, but strange as it sounds, that wasn't as traumatic for me as not wanting her."

When it finishes, Scarlett turns away. Above her right ear an orange light flashes. Her battery is losing charge; it will be flat soon. My heart aches for the poor little thing.

"I have a surprise, but you have to promise to be good. No more destroying my things or vandalising the walls."

I reach into my pocket. "Ta-dah!"

She whips around and stares at the cards of batteries in my hand. "What are they?"

"Batteries for your implants. I bought boxes of them for you."

She comes closer and examines them, then slaps my hand, sending the cards flying through the air. "They're the wrong batteries," she screams.

I pick them up. "No, honey. These are the right ones, the woman in the pharmacy told me. The label says *they are suit-*

able for cochlear implants and hearing aids. I made sure to get the right ones."

She removes her left implant from her ear and separates it into two pieces. The green blinking light goes out. She hands one piece to me.

"Where do they go?" I search for the place to put the small disc batteries, but there is nowhere.

"They're the wrong ones," she says. "There is nowhere to put them. You need a charger."

I don't have a charger. The website wouldn't sell me one unless I set up an account linked to a deaf child, certified by a medical professional.

"I didn't know they wouldn't work together."

"Let me go home," Scarlett screams, tears streaming down her face.

"Shush for a minute. Let me think."

"I hate you; I hate you; I hate you."

"Shut up and let me think. Can you hear like that, with just one implant?"

"Kind of. It's harder."

"Leave the other implant off while I figure this out. Save the power."

She puts the implant down in two pieces on the dresser beside her bed. Her right implant continues to flash orange, which will have to do for now.

18

KAREN

Day 2 – 18:00

I've been here for hours. Same Garda station, different room – the interview room.

There are two black globes on the ceiling. I expected a half-wall of a mirror, our every word and movement being observed and recorded, but the walls are bare. Two detectives sit opposite me in silence as I tear pieces from my empty polystyrene cup and pile them on the table in front of me.

DI Samantha Clarke clicks her fingers. "The telly – you were on the telly. That's where I know you from." She turns to her colleague. "That was putting my head away. What was it she was on?"

"*Good Morning, Ireland,*" I answer.

"That's it! You were talking about—"

"Prenatal and postnatal depression. I wish I hadn't gone on that program."

She raises an eyebrow.

"I didn't realise what I'd said until the interview was over, and then it was too late to fix. The abuse on social media was shocking. I lost friends both in real life and online. I was cancelled over one badly worded comment."

She sits forward. "Go on."

"I wasn't prepared for the level of hatred against me. Parents stopped meeting up with us, and the messages were horrendous. I could handle it while it was online, but when our apartment was vandalised, we were left with no choice but to move."

DI McGovern sits back in his chair. I try to lean back too, but my chair is fixed to the floor.

"How was Paddy through all of this?" he asks. He's dark and around the same age as Paddy, but taller and slimmer.

"My husband is a workaholic. He brings in the money. I take care of everything else. He never wanted me to be online in the first place, so I guess he felt justified in his warnings. He has no online presence, which I think is weird for a tech guy, but he says it's a—"

"Busman's holiday. And how are things between you both?"

"Dead." God, the truth comes easy. "But he adores Scarlett."

"And you? Does he adore you?" he asks.

"I don't know anymore, and I don't care. As I say, he's a good provider. He pays for all the extra support Scarlett needs. All private. All a fortune. I could never afford any of that. He's a good dad."

"Recently, has anything unusual happened?"

"Like what?"

"I don't know. Anything?"

I consider what my mother said. "There is something, but I don't know if it's relevant."

"Everything is relevant."

I lean forward, focusing on my hands. "Things between me and Paddy have never been great, but we thought maybe the new house... anyway, a few months ago I got it into my head that Paddy was having an affair. Nothing happened, but he was happier, more content, easier, if that makes sense."

There is a knock, followed by a woman opening the door. She calls the detectives outside. Alone, the black machine whirring in the corner, I remember telling my mother about my suspicions when I last visited. I didn't plan to, but when she poured the wine, I spilled.

"Would it be so bad if he was having an affair, darling?" she asked, dismissing my shock with a wave of her hand, as if it was nothing at all. "You can manage without him. Didn't we do perfectly well, just me and you?"

She had to be joking. I hated growing up in our two-person family. She expected too much of me from too young as she worked around the clock to keep food on the table. I didn't want to graft just to exist like my mother had.

As we sat looking out to sea, the sun setting, she lit a cigarette and asked if I loved him. I couldn't answer. It wasn't that simple.

"Karen, dear, life is short. I know you think you have your whole life ahead, but you will wake up one morning my age. You're a beautiful young woman; you have prospects."

I laughed at her bias. She was wrong. What prospects did I have? I hadn't worked for years, the whole industry had moved on, and Paddy was hiring people in their twenties. Sure, I could upskill, but that would take time and money, of which I had neither of my own.

"Why isn't he here?" she asked. "If he isn't having an affair."

"He's working."

She scoffed, the wine further loosening her already loose tongue.

"The new house needs decorating, Mam, and Scarlett's therapy. Someone needs to pay for it. Life costs."

She dragged from her cigarette, exhaling slowly. "If it weren't for Scarlett, would you care if he left? If the answer is no, then it's not fair to any of you to stay in this marriage."

"He loves her."

My mother slammed her fist on the table. "Rubbish. If you stay, what lesson are you giving your daughter? You have a decision to make. Stay in that marriage, or be happy."

I laid my head back against the chair. The truth made my head hurt. The wine and sun didn't help. Still, I grasped at straws. "But he's a great dad."

"Stop it! Everyone deserves to feel special, to feel loved, and Paddy O'Hara will never make you feel that way."

That hit a nerve, and the tears started to flow. I didn't like where this path was leading. "Where would we go if I left?"

She threw her arms out. "Here. Come here. We have this huge house, and Juan adores Scarlett. You'd have plenty of help."

I felt a flutter in my gut. A butterfly, a tiny butterfly of possibility. Hope. "I couldn't take Scarlett away from Paddy. He'd never agree to that. It wouldn't be fair."

"Paddy will survive."

I spent the rest of the week in turmoil, turning over the pros and cons of each choice. I could leave, come here, but that would mean taking Scarlett from her school, her therapies, her father. In the end, with all things considered, I decided to return home to my husband.

At the airport, my mother cried, the first time in my life, telling me her door was always open. She then took my hands in hers and kissed them.

"Fight for yourself, Karen. If not for you, for Scarlett. You are not only her mother but her role model. You are a woman, strong and beautiful; don't forget that."

As we took to the air, the beautiful city of Lisbon getting smaller below, I kissed Scarlett, who sat in my designated seat. My mother and her pipe dreams. Life didn't work like that. You made your bed, and you lay in it. I wanted to give Scarlett the best childhood, and that meant having both parents and access to the best therapies available. Scarlett fell asleep in my seat, her head on my knee. That's what a mother does. She gives up her seat.

Three hours later, the arrival gates opened, and Paddy waited with a huge bouquet and a pink heart balloon that bobbed above him, scanning the gates. He caught my eye and smiled, and I smiled back, but his whole face lit up when Scarlett ran to him. He picked her up and swung her around, then put his arm around me, unsure. "Are we good?"

"We're good," I said, and kissed him.

We returned to an immaculate house filled with fresh flowers that smelled like a new beginning. He must have spent the week cleaning, and I felt a huge pang of guilt before brushing it off and taking him to our bed.

My mother was wrong. We weren't perfect, but we were doing okay. We had no money worries, a beautiful house and a gorgeous girl who needed us both. That was more than most people could dream of.

The door of the interview room opens, pulling me back to the present, and the detective inspectors return.

"What time is it?" I ask.

"Half six," DI Clarke says.

"Her batteries will be dead," I say, incensed. "While we were wasting time in here, they were dying. She could be in the next room now and wouldn't hear me."

"Tell us about your medication," she says.

I put my head in my hands. "Again? I suffered from pre-

and postpartum depression. It left me with permanent anxiety. I took medication for it. That's it. Did you not hear what I said? Her batteries will be dead. She hates silence!"

She takes out her notebook. "And you stopped taking your medication when?"

"Oh my God, I told you. About a year ago."

"Around the time of the interview?"

"Just after it. I had to wake up."

"How have you been since?"

"Good. Still good since the last time you asked me a few minutes ago. And the time before that."

She moves her chair around; her leg brushes against mine when there is another knock. She goes to the door, now open, where another Garda whispers to her.

"She's in silence; my daughter is in silence," I cry to the Garda outside. DI McGovern looks at DI Clarke, who returns to her chair. "If Paddy knew where Scarlett was, would he tell us?" she asks.

"Yes. One thousand per cent yes. Wait – what kind of question is that?"

She stands. "Thanks for all your help, Karen. We're finished here for now."

"What's going on? What has this got to do with Paddy?"

She shrugs. "We don't know yet, but Paddy has come in for a chat in a highly agitated state, said he has important information, but wants to talk to us first. We'll get a car to bring you home."

I jump up and push past the detectives into the corridor. "Where is he? Let me speak to him."

"Not at the moment. We will let you know any updates we have, but right now you need to leave."

I open a door to an empty room, then another. "I'm not fucking leaving. If he has important information, I need to know it. I'm losing my mind here."

Then I see him, flanked by two Gardai and coming towards us. They see me and turn back, but I scream, "What's going on, Paddy?"

"I'm so sorry," he cries back before they bundle him into a room and close the door.

19

PADDY

Eight years ago

I never thought I would kiss, never mind sleep with someone like Karen Sullivan. With long blonde curls, an incredible body and intense blue eyes, from the moment she interviewed me for the role of senior programmer and laughed at my jokes, I was smitten. It was love at first sight, for me anyway. Now, a year later we sit in my car outside the Dublin maternity hospital, the rain belting off the car windscreen, while she clutches the scan and weeps.

"It's a miracle," I say, trying to contain my delight for her sake. Karen is carrying not one, but two of my babies.

"Paddy." She fishes a tissue from her bag. "We live in a one-bedroom city centre apartment on the fourth floor. We both work long hours. In what world is this a blessing?"

"In the world where we're making two little people. The apartment will be fine – the lift almost always works, and Fairview Park is a stone's throw away for walks and fresh air for the babies."

She sobs. "It's not just the apartment – you just don't get it."

"Hey, I do get it." I catch a tear rolling down her cheek. "It's tough and unexpected, but we're Team Fisher, remember? 'The A Team.'"

Last November she chose me to work on the Fisher project – a small piece of work for a large client. I was flattered and tried not to fantasise about the possibilities, but it was difficult being in such close proximity to her every day. We shared an office, and I didn't know what to say at first, but she was easy to talk to, and a lovely dynamic developed between us that thrived through working late nights and eating takeaways over our PCs. She was ambitious, and I was happy to be ambitious with her. The more time we spent together, the deeper my infatuation grew until she was all I thought of from morning to night. I was in love but dared not hope she felt something, too. That was too ridiculous.

"You're creative; I'm compliant, remember?" I chance a smile. They were her words when we delivered the project ahead of time. The company put on a free bar for the whole office. I showed up that night, brought my A game and made sure she had a drink in her hand at all times. We did shots and chasers and, at the end of the night, were the last two at the bar. As staff cleaned up around us, she put her head on my shoulder. I leaned in to kiss her and couldn't believe she responded, then agreed to come home with me.

The crazy, uninhibited goddess in my bed that night is a distant shadow of the one who now cries buckets beside me as the rain pours down on the car.

"Come on, this is fantastic news. Twins!"

"Twins," she cries. "I was struggling to get my head around one baby."

"I never had brothers or sisters to play with. I know you didn't either. It's scary, but we can do this—"

"No, Paddy. I don't think I can—"

"—and I wasn't sure I'd ever get to be a father. Our baby – babies will have a ready-made family. We'll be team O'Hara."

Until Karen, I didn't have the courage to talk to women, and sex was too much to contemplate. That changed the night I lost my virginity. In bed as in business, Karen under-promised and over-delivered, allowing me to follow her lead. The next morning, I brought her breakfast in bed. Fresh coffee, croissants and a rose, just like in the movies. She woke, rushed by me and brown-vomited on my cream bedroom carpet. I told her not to worry, but she couldn't get out of my apartment quick enough. She asked me not to tell anybody what happened between us the night before, that it had been a drunken mistake, and I agreed, fighting back the hurt and trying not to be offended. She was the best thing that ever happened to me.

Work was weird after that. We moved out of our shared office, and she was courteous but distant. She moved on to another project, and I joined two other men on data analysis. I wanted to tell them about our incredible night, but I respected Karen's wishes. They wouldn't have believed me anyway; I could hardly process it myself. I tried to contact her, but she wouldn't answer her phone, and emails were kept professional. Two months later, she called to meet in a local bar. I was hopeful, overjoyed, but when she arrived with a dour face, my heart sank. She was pregnant. I begged her to keep the baby, to give a relationship with me a try. No expectations, no commitment, just a trial run. She was reluctant, but I promised if she did, no matter the outcome, I'd be there for her and the baby to always take care of them.

She takes a deep breath. "Not Team O'Hara. Team Sullivan O'Hara."

I smile. "Team Sullivan O'Hara it is." It was an honour to have our names together. Telling the guys in the office that I slept with *The* Karen Sullivan was one of the best moments of my life. I know they thought I was spoofing but had to believe it when Karen confirmed we were expecting a baby together. I'll never forget their faces, a look of respect mixed with disbelief, as they surrounded her, hugging her and offering words of congratulations. They slapped my back and shook my hand and said I was a dark horse. Hell yes to Team Sullivan O'Hara.

She glances at the scan and bawls again. "This is a nightmare. I don't want to be a mother, responsible for growing these babies into adulthood and not messing them up. I can't do it. I can't."

The rain gets heavier and louder against the windscreen. I put my arm around her shoulder and pull her to me. "I'll be there every step of the way – I'm their daddy! People have been having babies since the beginning of time. Together, we'll do them proud."

"It's so much to process."

I lift her face. "Listen to me. The apartment, the room, we'll figure all that out when the time comes. We have good jobs, we can move to the suburbs, get a people carrier and become one of those smug couples. Right now, we have more than we need. Me, you, and our two little monkeys cooking in there." I put my hand on her bump. "Let's be happy today."

She sighs, and the crying subsides. "I want to be happy, Paddy, but I'm scared." She lays her head on my shoulder, and we sit in silence.

"I've got you. We'll be okay. When the babies come, you'll see there's nothing to worry about."

***

Two months later

"Two girls. Congratulations!" The sonographer prints a picture of our ultrasound scan at our next appointment.

"Elenora and Hope," I say.

"Lovely names. Have they any significance?" she asks Karen.

Karen stares at the monitor in silence.

"I'll leave you two to it," the sonographer says, glancing at Karen. "Congratulations again."

I'm over the moon. Two girls! We should be celebrating, but as we leave the hospital, my concern is growing. Karen hasn't opened her mouth since we got here. She's lost weight from the persistent vomiting, hyperemesis gravidarum they call it, but she could summon some enthusiasm for today. The obstetrician wanted her to remain in hospital to give her intravenous fluids but let her home on condition she go to bed and rest. It's all she ever does these days. She's been out sick from work for months now, and that project she was due to manage is starting.

My new role as project manager is challenging, but I love it. Still technical but more customer-facing than the back-end coding I was doing. I've invested in expensive tailored suits and shirts to appear more professional as I travel to London most weeks for one or two nights. When our manager told me of the travel required, I didn't want to take the position. I couldn't leave Karen at home alone when she was so sick, but she insisted I grab the opportunity and lay the groundwork for her. Our manager made it clear it's only a temporary arrangement until Karen returns, I'm simply keeping the bed warm for her, but this is my chance to show what I'm made of. The weekly trip was an inconvenience at first, but now I love it and look forward to the respite from the intense atmosphere of our home.

"I'll cancel tonight's trip and stay home with you." I help

her into her car. My car is in the garage. "You shouldn't be on your own."

"I'm fine. I need time, but I'll be fine." She drags her seat belt over her bump, huge on her narrow frame. "You go to London."

ICT put a lot of money and resources into wooing this client, but they're dragging their heels at signing the contract. If I return with that in the bag, a permanent promotion could be mine. "Only if you're sure. It might mean more money, and with two babies on the way now—"

"Oh, just drive, Paddy."

The rain eases, and as I wait for a break in the traffic to reverse onto Parnell Square, my work phone rings. News on the contract? I try to free it from the pocket in my trousers.

"Watch the fucking road!" a driver screams at us out his car window.

There is a break in the traffic as my phone rings again, and I let it ring out, but at the top of Parnell Street, it rings again. Karen tightens. I hope someone else hasn't got the client to sign; that could be my promotion on its head. Or maybe they are calling to tell me they'll sign. If so, I don't want to miss the call and someone else get the glory. I curse to myself and let it ring out.

The traffic lights turn red as we approach the T-junction ahead, and my phone rings again.

"Don't answer it, Paddy."

"I have to." I raise my body off the seat to free my phone, but my foot presses on the accelerator, sending the car hurtling onto the main road and into the path of an oncoming lorry. It smacks into Karen's door, spins us across the road and pushes the car into a wall side-on.

It's over in seconds. A tattooed bald man opens my car door. "You came out of nowhere."

He paces, head in his hands. "You came out of nowhere. I couldn't stop. What were you thinking? I never saw you."

"My partner – she's pregnant." Her side of the car is wedged against the wall. I lean across my seat. She's unconscious, blood trickling down the side of her face.

A crowd is gathering, and traffic builds. The lorry is sprawled across the whole road.

"Call 999," I call out. I reach to open Karen's safety belt. It's wet with blood, seeping through her shirtsleeve and saturating her cream linen trousers. I tap her face. "Karen, come on, wake up. Wake up."

Sirens fill the air within minutes as Gardai, ambulances and fire engines arrive. I answer their questions in a daze while they work.

"Yes, she's pregnant. Twins. Twenty-six weeks. My foot slipped."

Firefighters work to cut Karen out of the car, still unconscious, and I travel with her in the back of a speeding ambulance. For six long hours, they try to stop the bleeding, but, at twenty-six weeks, the girls are delivered by C-section, and Karen is put into an induced coma for the swelling on her brain. The girls are whisked to the Neonatal Intensive Care Unit and Karen brought to ICU.

In the family room that night, I check my phone to see who called earlier. It wasn't the client at all but a number I recognised as a scam caller doing the rounds, trying to extract credit card details.

Work was shocked when I called, and told me to take all the time I need.

Apart from a sore neck and a bruised rib, I escaped physically unscathed from the whole thing.

20

PADDY

Day 1 – 22:30
5 hours missing

This is a living nightmare. I thought life couldn't get worse, but I was wrong. My baby girl is missing, and I scan ditches, calling her name. Karen's phone rings, and when she mouths the words "my mother," I speed up until there is sufficient distance between us. Felicia Sullivan is hard work at the best of times. I can't handle her right now.

"Call friends and family," Karen said, but everyone would be gone home from the office for the weekend. I call John, the CEO, but he doesn't pick up, so I leave a message for him, then hover my finger over my mother's number before scrolling on through my address book. Conor. I could call him, but the last time we hung out was six years ago when he was my best man.

Karen had insisted on booking the Celtic Cellos for our wedding ceremony, who played over the friendly chatter of our guests as they filed into the candlelit room in the

Dromod Hotel. I wore an oatmeal linen suit with an open-necked white shirt. I felt good – I was a decent guy with a pensionable job, a charity direct debit and health insurance. The room fell silent, and the music stopped before starting a Celtic version of Canon in D. I turned to look. There she was, her long curls adorned with a white floral crown, a white fitted dress to the floor, holding a posey of red roses. As she walked towards me to start our lives together, holding the hand of our two-year-old daughter in a red dress, I felt like the luckiest man on the planet. In front of our slack-jawed colleagues, we said "I do." My mother wasn't there; she hadn't made any contact since that phone call to Karen, which also meant she had never seen Scarlett. If Da were still alive, he would have talked sense into her. Karen's mother was on safari in Kenya, but the people who mattered were present – our colleagues. The ones who had laughed now had to watch us tie the knot, and that was all that mattered.

Six years since I had someone whom I can call a friend. Nothing personal, work takes up so much time for us both, but it hurts to think there is nobody else I can call in the circumstances.

I follow the lane as it veers right towards the house. When I said goodbye to Scarlett this morning, she was asleep, and my mind was already on the weekend ahead. I didn't see her last night. Karen doesn't let me go to her when she's asleep, saying that I chose my own hours, and if I can't get home before bedtime, that's on me. It took five years for Scarlett to sleep through the night, sometimes waking up to ten times a night, which we discovered was tinnitus and the need to be beside someone for security. She still sleeps lightly. I kissed her goodbye on Thursday morning before I left for work; that was the last time I saw her awake. How did I let it come to this?

She wasn't visible in the CCTV of Karen's car returning on Thursday evening.

Karen wouldn't hurt Scarlett. No, there must be a logical explanation. Scarlett will show up. She has to. She's probably playing the hide-and-seek game of her life, but she's never lasted more than an hour with me before.

I walk further ahead of Karen. I warned her not to advertise her life on the internet for all to see, but she wouldn't listen. I was being dramatic, according to her. Overcautious with my self-enforced no-social-media policy. Even following that disastrous interview last year and the vitriol, she continued to post. The world and his mother know her movements, her favourite places and her habits. They know her favourite foods, activities and TV programs. Scarlett would go with anybody; she has no sense, no matter what Karen claims. If anyone harms a hair on her head, God help me, I will fucking kill them.

We're almost home when Karen catches up with me. I guide her through the crowd and into the house, but don't go inside with her. Instead, I turn and go back to the front gate.

"Can I have a word?" I ask Garda McCarthy. "In private."

"Sure, what is it?"

"Not here." We walk away from the house. "It might be something. I don't know if I should even mention it. It's a long time ago. It's, um..."

"Paddy, can you come here for a minute?" Karen is at the door, arms crossed.

"Paddy, what is it?" the Garda asks.

She glares at me, waiting.

"I'd better go."

"One moment." Garda McCarthy presses a card into my hand. "Call any time if you think of anything."

Saved by the bell, Karen's phone rings. I ask her not to accept Fintan Power's offer of help, but she does what she wants as usual. Upstairs in the office, I contemplate doing the decent thing and calling my mother before she hears the news from someone else. I find "Mam" in my phone and, holding my breath, press call, eight years since we last spoke, to hear, *"Sorry. This number is no longer in use."*

My first reaction is anger. She changed her number and didn't let us know, but then this is hardly a surprise from the woman who cut her only child from her life over a stupid name tradition. Still, she's getting on in years, and if even a fraction of the ailments she claimed to have materialised, she's probably in a nursing home, or worse still... No, if she died, someone would let me know.

Fintan Power arrives within minutes. The strange little man circles his hands in front of me, looking at me in a way that makes me nervous, like he's seeing into my brain. I follow him to the kitchen, where he observes every inch and holds his hands over every surface, feeling for Scarlett's aura. Rubbish. He lingers at the worktop, at the exact spot where we got carried away a few weeks ago. Wow, that was intense.

"I'm getting intense energy around here." He narrows his eyes at me. "Does that make sense to you?"

I feel myself redden. "Scarlett paints there; we cook there, I guess."

He circles his hands over the worktop. "No, that's not it. It's your energy... and there's something else."

My heart beats fast, but I don't react. He couldn't possibly know; he's feeding off my reactions. That's how these charlatans work, they micro-analyse your body language. All I have to do is act normal.

He watches me as he backs into the living room. "Where's Scarlett's bedroom?"

She shows him upstairs, and I stay downstairs with Helen.

"This is bullshit," I say.

"It's not my place to comment."

They come back downstairs, and we follow them outside and onto the patio, where Fintan unfolds a giant map of Ireland and stands on it, dangling a ring on a chain.

"What's he doing?" I whisper to Karen.

"Finding your daughter," he replies. He moves around the map, talking to the ring. I try to act breezy whenever he comes close to the white lounger where we had sex a few weeks ago.

He stops right beside it, his foot touching the base of the chair, and falls backwards, claiming he's picked up energy. I don't know how, but he's got this from me, read my reactions.

"Red. I'm feeling red." He closes his eyes. "Not the chair. Something else."

I tut, that would be my normal reaction, but my brain is on fire. "Her name is Scarlett, could that be it?"

He opens his eyes and paralyses me with a stare. "No. A different red. Does that make sense?"

I can't speak. *Rose.*

21

PADDY

Three weeks ago

Viewing this house was my idea, but it was Karen who fell in love with it. It reminded her of her home in Galway where she lived until her mother up and left, leaving her homeless. That evening, we put our apartment up for sale and made an offer on the house, which was accepted immediately. It was hard to believe this idyllic old farmhouse cost less than our city apartment, leaving money to decorate and kit it out.

At first, life was better in Westmeath, and although my commute to Dublin is over an hour each way, the air is clearer, and Karen was in better form. Scarlett gets to swim in the open water and play outside in a garden for the first time in her eight years of life.

Happy wife, happy life. She loved returning to the countryside. Being from Wexford Town, I'm more used to the urban life but fell into life and its easier pace with ease. That's when I'm not working, which is a rarity these days. Karen was pleasant until she became hormone crazy, snooping around, accusing me of ignoring her and having affairs, and following me.

I am having an affair, but she doesn't know that. I've been careful. No pictures on phones, no emails, definitely no social media. No credit card bills, phone calls only at pre-arranged times. Careful.

I was so lucky to meet Rose when I did because, at home, things are worse than ever. Karen never gets off my case, accusing me of never being here, of working too hard, of being neglectful of both her and Scarlett, but when I come home, all she does is nag or, worse, gives me the cold shoulder. It's like living with a stranger, and a mental one at that. If it weren't for Scarlett, I would be long gone.

I put up with a lot for Scarlett's sake, but when Karen claims I have no interest in her life, I fight back. It's Karen who leaves me out of the loop, keeping information from me and excluding me from decisions about my daughter. Yet she doesn't complain when I hand over the money to pay for them all.

I no longer know who my wife is or what she wants. I don't think she does either, and more than that, I no longer care. I'm in love with someone else.

In the midst of all of this misery and tension, my heart was stolen by the wonderful, captivating, fabulous Rose, who lies in my bed beside me.

Last Sunday morning, I came into the bedroom to find Karen packing a suitcase. "I can't live like this anymore. I'm taking Scarlett to my mother's house to get some space."

"For how long?"

"I don't know. I need time and space to think."

"Are you leaving me?"

"I don't know."

"How will I see Scarlett?"

She narrowed her eyes. "Always about Scarlett. Never

about me. I'm so tired of being second best to her, a child. Paddy, I am a person. I am dying here, forgotten."

"You need to go back to work. I can put in a word for you. I'm sure they'd take you back in ICT," I said. We had this argument so many times.

She came close to my face. "Who will bring Scarlett to her appointments? Who will mind her while we both commute to Dublin? Who will parent her while we work from morning to night? No, Paddy, I don't need a job. I need to be valued and seen by my own fucking husband."

"I don't always feel valued. Do I not deserve to feel valued, or is it only you?"

She folds clothes and puts them into the case. "Then maybe you should use the time to think about what you want too."

I knew what I wanted. Rose and Scarlett. I was very clear in what I wanted. Getting it was a different matter.

"Don't try to contact me under any circumstances. I need to not be around you for I don't know how long." Those were her last words before leaving in the taxi that afternoon to catch a last-minute, expensive flight, paid for on my credit card, to her mother's villa in Portugal.

Since then, apart from the worry of her taking Scarlett, I'm living the dream. Each evening after dark, Rose slips through the back gate. We can't risk the Devlins at the top of the road seeing her. It was a great move resisting the security cameras in our house.

The time passes too fast. Blissful nights and hard early morning partings to go to work are made bearable in the knowledge that I will see Rose that evening. We can't travel together in case we're seen. Long lazy dinners, late-night chats. I thought I knew what happiness was, but I hadn't a clue until I met Rose. I never want this to end.

I'm making toast in our messy kitchen when my phone

beeps. A text from Karen. It's six days since they left, and I haven't tried to contact her as per her request.

We will be home tomorrow. Flight arriving in Dublin 15:30.
Be there if you want to give us a second chance x

The message, the second chance, the x at the end of the message meaning... what? She wants to try again? I don't want her to come back, but the anticipation of seeing Scarlett in just over twenty-four hours fills me with joy.

Bare-legged and carrying a paperback book, Rose saunters by in my blue shirt. Last night we cooked a full Italian meal, which we enjoyed with wine. So much wine.

She kisses my cheek. "Come outside. It's a beautiful day, and for once we've no work."

"I'll clean up a little first." Every work surface has dishes of half-eaten food piled high. Karen would lose her shit if she saw it.

Rose steps out to the garden. "Come on, we can do that later."

She lies on a sun lounger on the patio, her bare legs stretched out. She twirls a strand of dark hair, engrossed in her book. I need to find a way to be with both my favourite girls – Rose and Scarlett. I need them both. If I leave Karen, she could go to Portugal to live with her mother, and take Scarlett with her. She has nobody keeping her here, and Felicia has made it clear she would love to have them both there. It's not fair. I work my ass off to give my daughter the best life, yet I'm powerless to keep her here with me.

I carry black coffee and buttered toast into the garden. On the two loungers, side by side we lie, Rose engrossed in her book.

Resting my head on my hands, I close my eyes. "I wish this were my life. I wish you were my wife."

She bursts out laughing. "You're a poet and you don't know it."

I laugh too, but she continues way longer than me, the tears streaming down her face. "Ah, brilliant."

"Ha, paralyses, very funny. Glad I amuse you. But I do though."

She's still chuckling, but when I take her hand, she stops.

"I love you. I love you so much."

She puts the book down and raises an eyebrow. "Do you? Do you really love me?"

"Yes, I do. You know I do."

She considers me, then joins me on my lounger, straddling me. Leaning down to me, her hair falling on my chest, she whispers, "Then leave your wife." Her voice is hoarse, her lips brushing mine.

I kiss her. "I can't leave."

"Why not?" She kisses me harder.

"Scarlett," I manage.

She takes my shorts off. "Bring her with you. We'll set up somewhere new. I should be coming into money very soon, a lot of it. We can go anywhere we like."

I pull my blue shirt over her head to discover she is naked underneath. "I told you I'd like nothing more, but it can't happen. I've always been honest."

She shakes her hair out. "People split up all the time and get to see their children. You can't live your life miserable with Karen for the sake of your child when you could be happy with me."

Sitting up in all her beautiful glory, the lake glistening in the distance behind her, it aches to think of a moment without her.

"You are so beautiful. I need you." I nuzzle her neck.

"Then leave her."

At that moment, with the lake lapping and sun shining, I

know she's right. People have broken up since time began. Life happens, people change, although saying that about Karen is an understatement. I have to find my courage.

"Yes. I'll leave my wife. I want to be with you."

She cries out, and soon we're enjoying each other, the outdoors and danger removing any remaining inhibitions. Different from the cold, controlled copulation this house is used to. I sit up and pull her onto me when a loud clunk comes from behind. Christy Devlin stands watching, the wheelbarrow on its side in front of him, but I'm too far gone to stop. I bite into Rose's shoulder, stifling my inevitable moan, but she has her back to Christy and misinterprets my actions, becoming more animated.

"Stop." I pant as she becomes increasingly vocal. "Christy's here." I push her off me. "Christy's here," I say again, but by the time she turns, he is gone. I get dressed and run out after him to see his car disappearing up the lane.

This is a disaster. In my bedroom, Rose packs her toiletries into her backpack. "Calm down. It's hardly ideal, but, Paddy, this could be the best thing to happen to us if it forces our hand. Talk to Christy. Explain that this isn't a fling. Tell him we're serious."

"I don't know if I can face him. If I lose Scarlett..."

She stops packing. "Paddy, don't you dare back down. You haven't come this close to come this close."

When she leaves through the back gate and I'm in the house alone, the implication of what Christy witnessed hits me like a steam train. There is no way back now. An hour later, I knock on the Devlins' door, shaking and setting the dog barking.

Mrs Devlin welcomes me into her stifling hot house, a knowing smile on her face. The fire blazes up the chimney while a black cat sleeps on the table. An Alsatian dog barks at me from the kitchen.

"Be quiet, Maxi! Don't worry about her; her bark is worse than her bite," Mrs Devlin says and places a plate of buttered brack and a pot of tea on the table without disturbing the cat.

My stomach is doing flips. I can't eat, but I accept the offer of tea to be polite.

"Is Christy here?" I stir the tea, my hand trembling, trying to sound breezy.

"He's outside, tricking at some piece of machinery. I'll get him."

Through the biscuit-colour net curtain on the tiny red window, I see her talking to him in the yard. The dog creeps closer to me, growling, as the old couple argue in the yard. Christy glances back towards the room. I shudder at what he witnessed and its implications. His shoulders slump as she whispers to him, and he comes towards the house, wiping his hands with a yellow stained towel. Patting the dog's head as he passes, he sits opposite me at the table, without making eye contact, and Mrs Devlin takes the chair beside him. I focus on my tea, trying to ignore the short black hair floating on the top.

"I was hoping to talk to Christy on his own," I say to Mrs Devlin.

"We have no secrets, dear. I know what happened with you and your fancy woman." She softens her voice. "What are you playing at, at all?"

"You don't understand. She's not my fancy woman. She is – I – I love her."

Christy slams his fist on the table, startling the cat, which leaps from the table. "You fool. What about your wonderful wife and daughter? Did you think about them?"

"If it weren't for thinking about them, I'd be long gone."

Christy's eyes water. "Well, aren't you the great fella? And you'll tell Karen what you've been at behind her back, will you?"

I look away.

"Pathetic." Christy stands and leaves the room, the dog following him.

"Paddy," Mrs Devlin says, "you've had your head turned. A demanding job, a home life that is hard, a child with a lot of needs. An attentive woman comes along, sweeps you off your feet and offers you an escape from reality. You wouldn't be the first and you won't be the last to be tempted. But trust me, it's a fantasy, and it won't end well. I've been around the block enough times to know."

She smiles, her kind face creasing.

"You don't know her. It's not like that."

She sits back. "Maybe not, but let's tease this out. You leave your wife, you fight over custody, you poison your child's mind against her mother, and she poisons hers against you. The child develops more issues, and the woman who started it all gets sick of your bitterness and leaves you – alone with no wife and a messed-up child. Is that what you want?"

Christy comes back in. "We're talking in private," she says, and he goes back to the kitchen, muttering under his breath.

She brushes a tear from her cheek. "I'm speaking from experience. Christy had an affair. Oh, it's a long time ago now. We got back together, obviously, but not before we half-destroyed each other. The damage was done. Freddie couldn't wait to get away from us and couldn't have picked somewhere further away than Australia. Trust me, you don't want to live with that on your conscience. End it before lasting damage is done."

I can't imagine Christy with another woman, but Mrs Devlin's expression tells me she's serious.

"This is not the same thing. You love Christy. My wife hates me."

"And you know that for sure, do you? Have you asked her or assumed that?"

I don't answer.

"What if, and hear me out. What if she still loves you, but you've neglected each other? Isn't it worth finding out if there's a chance to reignite things with your wife before doing something with that woman that you can't come back from?"

"It's already too late to come back. Karen doesn't love me."

"It's not too late. End the affair now, and you can avoid a world of pain. For all of you."

My heart sinks as I feel my future drifting away in front of my eyes, a door closing. "And if I end it, you won't say anything to Karen?"

"I won't, but I can't speak for himself." She nods to the kitchen, where Christy is drying dishes. "Go talk to him; sort it out. He's a good man." She puts her hand on my arm. "And you are too."

I step into the tiny kitchen, where Christy is drying dishes. I cough to get his attention. He doesn't react, so I cough louder.

He slams a pot into the press without turning. "You should have cancelled me this week instead of letting me come and witness that abomination. You've put me in a terrible predicament."

"I'm sorry. I didn't know you were due to come. Why didn't you leave when you heard us?"

He points to his ears. "Hearing loss, son. You, of all people, should understand. I got an awful shock." He reddens. "Shameful behaviour. So you're leaving your wife for her, are you?"

"I don't know. Are you going to tell Karen what you saw?"

"If you swear to end it right now and to care for that beautiful child and wonderful wife of yours, then you have my word that I will never say a thing about it."

"When are they home?" Mrs Devlin asks, standing in the doorway.

"Tomorrow night."

She takes the bucket and mop from the cupboard in the corner. "I'll help you get the house ready for her; clean it up, clear the air. Then you will buy the most expensive bouquet you can find, meet them both at the airport and forget all about this nonsense."

Rose will be devastated, but she'll understand.

Christy picks up a bread knife with a weathered hand and waves it at me. "If I ever see you tricking with that woman or anyone else again, you will have me to deal with. Understand?"

"Loud and clear. I truly appreciate you doing this for me."

He slams the knife into the cutlery drawer. "Not for you." He looks me up and down. "You're a disgrace."

"Everyone's allowed one mistake," she says.

He picks up a plate.

Mrs Devlin takes bottles of cleaning products from the press. "The crowd in that house before you were tyrants," she tells me. "Tortured us. We were in the Garda station more times than the church. In the end, it was the CCTV that caught them acting the maggot. We couldn't take the risk of having bad neighbours again, not at our age."

"What she's saying is that it's in our interest as much as yours to keep you here. Consider yourself lucky," Christy says. He lays the towel down.

Mrs Devlin follows me home in her car. She opens all the windows and cleans the house from top to bottom with the products she brought, even though we have all of them here, giving me orders and sending me into Mullingar on errands. By night-time, the house is clean, fresh and stunning, and the fridge and freezer are stocked.

"Now." She surveys her work. "A clean start."

The next day at the airport, Karen beams as she comes through arrivals. Scarlett runs to me, and I lift her up. "I missed you so much. I love you, Daddy." She wraps her arms around me, covering my face in kisses.

Karen follows, looking better and... happy? I put my arm around her, and she doesn't pull away. "Are we good?"

"We're good," she says and kisses me in a way that surprises me. As we walk through the terminal, Scarlett tells me all about her holiday at breakneck speed, full of excitement, and Karen takes my hand. We pass departures, and my heart breaks at the thought of no more secret trips away, real or pretend. The end of an era. The end of Rose.

That night I make quiet, comfortable love to my wife and afterwards hold her in my arms as she drifts to sleep. I promised her I would be there for her always, and a promise is a promise.

22

PADDY

Day 1 – 10:00

A knock on the door of our hotel room wakes me. Room service. I pour a cup of coffee from the pot and place it on the table beside the king-size bed where Rose sleeps. I sit on the edge, and she stirs.

"Good morning, beautiful," I say.

She stretches out and yawns. "I must have nodded off. You, sir, are exhausting."

We've been here since half seven this morning. I hand her the coffee.

"What did I ever do to deserve you?" she asks.

"I'm the one who lucked out. Getting to spend the entire weekend here, with you." I put my hand on her thigh.

"Mmm. You are insatiable... and I love it." She takes a sip. "This is good coffee. Exactly the way I like it."

I know she likes her coffee black, scrambled eggs and brown bread for breakfast, that she doesn't wear earrings, and she snores. I know her. I trace my fingers down her body, careful to avoid her appendectomy scar. Not as tall or slim as

Karen, but no part of me would rather be with anyone else. Considerate, kind and uninhibited; in a different life she would be the woman I share my house with, she who would mother my children, but I met Karen first. It wasn't written in the stars; there is no fairy godmother to wave her magic wand and reverse time to make that happen.

My mother would adore Rose and be thrilled if I left Karen, but I can't.

I'll always be there, that's what I promised Karen, but people change. The thought of how close I came to losing Scarlett makes me shudder. I hope Rose will understand that we have to keep our relationship secret for now. I'm sure she will. I have always been upfront with her.

"Hey, what's up?" She rubs my arm.

"You know I love you."

"I love you too." She looks into my face, and her brown eyes deepen to black. "Paddy, what's going on?"

I lie beside her. "I don't know how to put this."

She sits up. "Don't tell me you're having second thoughts—"

"I can't leave Karen. She'll take Scarlett to Portugal, and I'll never see her."

"Jeepers, Paddy, I don't believe this."

"Scarlett."

"And I'll help you fight for custody. You're her dad. Hell, take her with you!"

"No judge in the land will take Scarlett from her stay-at-home mother and give custody to me, a dad who works around the clock. Karen will get custody, move abroad, and I'll only see my daughter at Christmas and holidays. I couldn't bear that."

She turns away from me, and I kiss her shoulder. "I love you, Rose. I mean every word. You and me, we're a far better match than Karen and I ever were."

"You're never going to leave her, are you?" she asks under her breath.

"It's not that simple."

She whips around. "Answer. The. Question. Are you ever going to leave your wife? Yes or no. Don't mess me around any longer."

I shake my head. "I can't."

She whips back the sheet and throws her legs out of the bed. The gorgeous atmosphere from ten minutes ago has disappeared.

"Rose, please. We can still see each other."

"I have to get going." She scoops her underwear from the floor.

"Don't do this. I hate it as much as you. I can't leave Scarlett, but I need you too. Why can't we stay as we are?"

"That's called having your cake and eating it, Paddy, and this cake just ran out."

"No, Rose, listen. Do you know how many times I have come home to find Scarlett alone while her mother is on the phone or laptop? That's not right. What would happen if they left the country? My little girl needs me, her father. I can't abandon her."

She pulls her striped sweater over her head. "I'm going for a walk before I say something I regret."

"Rose, please." I pull her to me. "We can be happy like this. Just me and you."

She shirks me off. "Goodbye, Paddy."

"You're not being fair. Is this not enough for you? You knew I was married when we got together. You said it was enough."

"I never said that." Her jaw tightens, and I think for a moment she's going to hit me, but then she sniffles, gathers herself and heads for the door. "I need time to figure things out. I'll be back later this evening when I calm down."

She leaves. I take a long shower, then wrap up in the thick towelling robe and fall asleep. I wake to an empty room. As the hours pass by, my anxiety grows. It killed me to see her in such pain, but I had to be honest. I am always honest with her. We need to talk about how I'm stuck between her wants and needs and Karen; my life is all about what they want. Surely, I matter too, but she doesn't come back. She isn't answering her phone either. She's angry, but she could have told me she wasn't coming back instead of leaving me waiting here like a fool all day. I throw my clothes into my case. I'm not staying here for the weekend, not able to leave the room for fear of being seen. I curse her as I leave without checking out, she's already paid for the room, and formulate an excuse as to why I'm home when I should be in London.

The house is silent as I enter. It's never quiet. Karen must have brought Scarlett out to the lake. I stay still, listening for any sound, but it is silent. I'll try to call Rose one more time and then forget about it until after the weekend. Even though she's pissed me off, I hate leaving things on a bad note, and I'm annoyed. I was always honest with her, always. I climb the stairs, miles away in my mind, and pass the office doors when a chilling scream comes from the office.

23

PADDY

Day 2 – 11:30
18 hours missing

I wash my hands in the downstairs bathroom and splash my face with cold water. I haven't slept a wink. The house is empty now except for the two of us, and after a night of searching, we are no further along. Karen has truly lost it, convinced that there's clues in Scarlett's paintings. She made us look like fools live on national TV, showing that stick-figure picture, claiming it's an identi-fit of an abductor, as if she's fricking Columbo, and calling in a clairvoyant. She's not well, but my priority is my daughter and getting her home.

During the appeal, I may as well have been invisible. Every question was for Karen. Not one journalist in the room asked or even acknowledged me, the father.

My stomach growls. I wish that woman, Vera, would hurry back with the coffee and food. I glance in the bathroom mirror and see an old, unshaven man looking back. My eyes linger on the medicine cabinet beside me. Karen's behaviour has been increasingly erratic; I wonder... On the shelf where she keeps her pills is the box in its usual spot. I pick it up to find it half-full, but when I turn it over to check the date on the label, it says last August. We didn't even live here last August. There are no other boxes of her pills in this cabinet. I fetch her black handbag from the coat stand in the hallway, the one she always carries with her, and bring it back to the bathroom, spilling its contents onto the closed toilet seat. My stomach drops. Amongst the cards, make-up and other bits lies a folded bundle of familiar cream A5 sheets. I open it to find multiple unfilled prescriptions.

She moves upstairs, and I gather her belongings back into her bag, replacing it where I found it, then go out into the garden. I call Garda McCarthy and tell him what I had set out to tell him before Karen interrupted us earlier.

Do I believe my wife could hurt our daughter? I don't know; I have seen her in dark places. She's like a different person when she's like that, one who shouldn't be taking care of a child. Rose is far more stable. Speaking of Rose, I desperately want to talk to her right now; she is so logical and calm; she would set my mind at ease and help me through this. She still hasn't made contact, and she is not answering my calls. Who would have another number for her? It's a long shot, but I search for the company she works for and call the number on-screen.

"Exception-L Solutions. Kate speaking."

"Hello, Kate. I was wondering if you could help me. I'm an, ahem, friend of Rose Hayes, who works in your childcare centre there, and I need to contact her urgently. Family emergency. I know she doesn't work Saturdays, so I'm wondering if you would have a home number for her?"

What I'm asking is illegal, but I hope that a Saturday receptionist mightn't know GDPR or care, so what happens next throws me.

"Rose Hayes is here today; I'll put you through."

I barely have my breath back when the call is answered.

"Rose Hayes. Can I help you?"

"Rose, it's me. Paddy." I glance over my shoulder.

"Paddy who?" she asks in a Dublin accent. Not her soft lilt and a different timbre.

"Come on, Rose, stop messing. It's Paddy."

"Who is this?" she demands. It's not Rose.

"I think I have the wrong person. Are there possibly two Rose Hayes working there?"

"Paddy who?" she demands again. I glance back to the kitchen, where Karen stands, staring out at me.

"Hello? Hello?" Karen approaches, and I end the call. She hands me her phone.

"It's my mother. She wants to talk to you."

Felicia, the last thing I need.

"Paddy, are you out of Karen's earshot?"

I walk down the garden. "Yes, I am, Felicia."

"Excellent. Paddy. Now, it kills me that I can't be there for my daughter, and I know we have had our differences, but I'm trusting you to take my place and look after her. I'll keep trying to find a flight, but, in the meantime, I'm counting on you to keep me updated on events. Do you understand?"

"Yes, Felicia." It kills her she can't be there for her daughter? How ironic.

"Take care of your wife. She needs you."

———

THE DETECTIVES LEAVE with Karen in the back of their unmarked car, and I follow up the lane in my Merc. I drive slowly to avoid all the people searching along the lane, and as I pass the Devlins, Christy steps out in front of the car. I slam on the brakes and roll down the window. "What are you doing, Christy? You could have got yourself killed."

He doesn't move. "Why are they taking Karen away?"

"They want to talk to her. Can I get by?"

He walks around to my car door and leans in the window. "You wouldn't have had anything to do with that, would you?"

"What? No. She's gone to the station for a chat, that's all."

He points his finger at me. "I love that girl like a daughter. I won't stand by and watch anything happen to her."

I step out of the car. I'm taller than the older man, but he puffs out his chest and stands his ground. The dog bounds around the corner from the backyard and snarls. Christy grabs a hold of her collar, but she pulls against him.

"Christy, please. I have to get by. I need to get to the station."

"Did you tell them about your bit on the side?" he spits, his face contorted.

"No. Why would I? Sure, that's all finished. She's gone."

He steps closer to me, the dog snarling, dripping saliva. "The question is, why wouldn't you? Are you hiding something? The way I see it, your child is missing, and you're withholding information."

"Christy, she's gone. Listen to me. It's pointless saying anything about that because it has nothing to do with Scarlett, and I'll stand to lose everything."

Christy continues, "I checked the CCTV. That woman in your house never passed our house when she was keeping you company while your family was away, which means she came in through your back gate. Have you told them that?"

I swallow.

Christy slaps the car bonnet, startling me, and the dog breaks into a fit of barking. "You're an idiot, that's what you are, son. A selfish idiot. I told you to end it. I warned you something bad would happen."

"I did end it."

He's right up in my face. "You're a liar. A liar and a weakling," he hisses.

"Takes one to know one," I snap, and Christy's mouth falls open.

"Yes, Christy, I know about your own misdemeanour. Give me two hours to prove she's not involved. That's all I ask. Two hours. If I can't, I'll tell the Gardaí everything. You know, more than most, how this relationship, that is now over, could destroy everything."

He steps back, huffing and panting, and I sit back in the car. Christy leans in the open window. "Two hours, son, not a minute more or I go to the police myself."

MY WORLD IS CLOSING in as I drive down the motorway to the IFSC, the Merc wanting to go faster than the hundred kilometres per hour, but the last thing I need is to be pulled over for speeding. I have to find Rose. I make a mental note to drop in or pick something up in the office, to give myself an alibi. The place I'm interested in is just around the corner from ICT. Exception-L.

At reception, I'm buzzed in by a glamorous young brunette with a headset. She doesn't acknowledge me as I cross the polished marble foyer.

"I'm looking for a Rose Hayes, please" – I check her name tag – "Kate?"

"Can I say what it is in connection with?" she asks, focused on her screen and tapping her keyboard with long manicured red nails.

"It's private," I say.

She raises an eyebrow and continues tapping. "Hello?

Rose, there is a man who wants to speak to you. Says it's private."

She keeps her eyes on the screen while talking to Rose through her headset. "Yes, I'll stay here." She nods towards the lime green seats in the bright reception area. "Rose is coming down now. Take a seat."

I flick through the *Financial Times* sprawled across the low glass coffee table. Rose Hayes is in the building, and Rose Hayes works here; there must be some misunderstanding with the last phone call.

The lift pings, and out walks a tall young woman with blonde short hair in a navy scrubs-like uniform and white runners. She chats with the receptionist before approaching me. "You want to talk to me?"

Rose Hayes, her name tag says, in a rainbow of colours and comic sans font.

"Is there another Rose Hayes here?"

She regards me with an expression of curiosity. "Did you ring here earlier?"

"Yes, I did. I—"

"Listen, pal, I don't know what's going on, but I'm Rose Hayes. Hold on, do I know you?"

I can't breathe. I make my excuses, apologise, and get out of there as quick as I can. Outside, the streets are deserted. The busy business Monday–Friday atmosphere evaporated. The shutters are down on the café where we first met. I run back across the road and bang on the glass of Exception-L with my fists. The receptionist rolls her eyes and buzzes me in.

"Yes?" she asks as I cross the reception floor.

"Do you have CCTV?"

"We have indeed. Hey, you're the man whose child is missing? From the telly?"

"Um, yes, that's me. Can I see the CCTV?"

"We don't allow—"

"My child is missing. Please. This once, make an exception."

She presses her vivid pink lips together, then calls through the open door behind her. "Jason? Can you come out here for a minute? There's a man here you might be able to help."

"Tell 'im to come on through," a deep London voice calls back, and I'm welcomed into the tiny security office behind reception by a man in his fifties. I take a seat beside him and a panel of screens showing multiple views of the front entrance, the lobby and the car park. He swivels around.

"What can I do you for, mate?"

"I need to see your CCTV. I'm looking for someone who works here."

"Sorry, mate, no can do without a warrant. GDPR."

"Please, I'm desperate."

He sucks in air. "Nah, I can't. I wish I could help you, but it's more than my job's worth. Come back with a warrant, and you can have all the CCTV you want. Who are you looking for?"

"Rose Hayes."

"You just met her in the lobby."

"It's not her."

"Maybe you got the wrong name. Have you an address?"

"I don't."

He whistles. "A picture?"

"No picture. But if you could check the CCTV, I'd know her straight away. She comes in around 8:30am every morning. I'd only be two minutes."

"Sorry, pal, can't help you. Come back with a warrant, and there won't be a problem."

24

PADDY

Day 2 – 17:30
24 hours missing

On the north quays of Dublin city centre, the sun beats in the windscreen of my car. I'm stuck in Saturday stop-start, stop-start traffic and losing my mind. All the shoppers and tourists out and about on such a fine day. Any other time, I would relish heavy traffic as an excuse to ring Rose, sharing details of our lives and enjoying each other's conversation. It did more than help pass my commute; it made the commute the highlight of the day. When I think back on all those deep conversations, it occurs to me: I talked, and she listened, always interested in what I had to say. Interested in me. I beep the horn at a teenage girl running across the road just as there is a break in the traffic.

"Save it for your wife," she screams, and gives me the two-finger salute.

My head is wrecked. Where is Rose? She isn't answering her phone, and she doesn't work where she claimed to.

Why would she say she did, and why would she take someone else's identity? I've never been to her house, but I'm starting to doubt that she lives in Drogheda and works in childcare at all. Was our first meeting a happy coincidence at all?

The traffic stops yet again, and I switch on the radio as the news starts.

The mother of missing child Scarlett O'Hara arrived at Mullingar police station this afternoon escorted by two uniformed Gardai, where she remains. They say she's helping them with their inquiries. The eight-year-old child was reported missing from her home yesterday evening at 7pm.

I switch it off and pray for the traffic to clear, which it does past Houston station. Passing Kinnegad, my phone rings, and I answer through the in-car system. "Paddy speaking."

"Hello, Paddy, it's Helen." Does she never clock off? "I'm here at your house. Can you come back? We want to ask you a few more questions."

"I'll be there in twenty."

As I turn off the N4 and down our lane, Christy is waiting outside his house. I pull into his driveway and step out of the car.

"Time's up, buddy," he says.

I break down. "I've been a fool, Christy. An utter fool."

"That you have, son, but you need to tell them everything. Tell them who she is."

My hands shake. "I don't know who she is. She lied to me. I know nothing about her. Nothing. I don't know her real name, where she works or where she lives or nothing."

"You idiot," Christy says. "What the hell have you done?"

THE TWO DETECTIVES who called to our house for Karen earlier now sit opposite me. I asked Helen to bring me to the Garda station but couldn't bring myself to tell her why.

"So," DI Samantha Clarke says, "you wanted to talk to us."

"I haven't been completely honest, but I want to fix that now. For the last nine months I've been in a relationship with a woman called Rose Hayes."

DI McGovern whistles. "That's a big chunk of information to not mention. Why now?"

"Rose told me she lives in Drogheda and works in the crèche in a company called Exception-L in the IFSC. She's not answering her phone, and I'm just back from the IFSC. Someone called Rose Hayes works there, but it's not her, so it's likely a lie. I don't know what the truth is."

DI Clarke leans forward. "You never went to her home or workplace in all that time?"

I shake my head. "I was careful."

She raises an eyebrow. "And you had a sexual relationship with this woman?"

"Yes. We went to hotels mostly. And my car. We had a schedule."

"What was your schedule?"

"Monday and Friday mornings we met in my car in ICT car park, out of view of the cameras. Wednesday evening after six we'd meet in the Premier Inn, Dublin Dockside, and some weekends we'd stay in the Radisson Airport Hotel."

"What dates were these?"

"Every week for the last eight months."

"Do you have a photo of this woman?"

"No. At the start of the relationship we made a deal. No photos and no social media – for obvious reasons."

DI McGovern raises an eyebrow. "Did you never google her? I know the first thing I do when I meet someone is a search."

"See, that's the thing, we both hate social media. Because she worked with children, she preferred to stay offline. My wife lives her life online, and it was refreshing to be with someone different. Someone who was in the moment, not always checking their phone. I didn't question it, and as for me, well, I'm surrounded by computers all day, the last thing I want to do when I come home is to go online."

"Can you give us a description of this woman?"

"Dark brown straight hair to her shoulders. About five feet three or four. Nicely built. Brown eyes. Pretty."

"Any unusual features?" DI Clarke asks.

"No, not that I can think of. She was pleasant to look at."

"In this time, did she show interest in Scarlett?"

I consider. "She never met Scarlett, but I spoke about her all the time. She never minded and always listened. When we spoke about me leaving Karen, she encouraged me to bring Scarlett with me. She knew I couldn't leave without her."

"Who would bring the conversation up, about you leaving?"

"I would." I think back to all the conversations. "I don't – I don't know."

"Did she have children herself?"

"No, no children, but there was something. She had stretch marks exactly like Karen's on her abdomen and a scar on her right side that she attributed to an appendectomy, but she got anxious if I touched it or" – I look to the ground – "kissed it."

"Is there anything else that struck you as strange?"

"Not until this weekend. She booked a hotel room. We were there since Friday morning, then had a massive argument. She left, saying she'd come back by evening time but didn't. I went home and haven't been able to contact her since."

"What was the argument about?"

"I told her I couldn't leave Karen. She was hurt, but I thought she'd come back to the room when she cooled down. Can you find her?"

He rubs his jaw. "Can we find a woman whose name you don't know, whose picture you don't have, of average appearance and pleasant looking?"

"There is one thing. Karen and Scarlett took a holiday a few weeks ago. Rose stayed in our house for the week they were gone, so I'm sure her DNA will be all over the house and the garden furniture, although – shit! We cleaned thoroughly after she left."

"Who's we?"

"Mrs Devlin, our neighbour, helped."

"Wonderful. We should still be able to get some traces."

"There's one more thing. She came in through the back gate from the lake. I gave her the key."

"She had the key?" DI Clarke asks. "This person who you haven't mentioned until now, who isn't who she says she is, who you don't know where she lives, had the key? That's a lot of coincidences, wouldn't you say?"

"I know how this looks, but you have to believe me. Check the hotel; check their records. She has to have paid by card. I'll know her from the CCTV. Ask at Exception-L, her company, although that's probably pointless. It seems she doesn't work there. She must have made a copy of the key to the back gate."

DI McGovern clicks his pen. "What's her car reg? You must know that."

"She doesn't drive."

"But how did she get to the lake?"

"I suppose the bus?"

He exhales. "Before I give this information to the team, is there anything you want to tell us? Anything you want to get off your chest?"

"This is everything."

He squeezes his eyes closed and pinches the bridge of his nose.

DI Samantha Clarke speaks. "Paddy, I know you're a good man. You say you've been unfaithful, which, God knows, doesn't make you the first or the last. If this is a false story, you need to tell us right now before our guys lose valuable time and energy on a false lead. If there's anything going on, it would be a good time to come clean. Put an end to this while you still can."

I put my head in my hands. "Honestly, this is what happened."

"Okay, Paddy," she says. "We'll request CCTV from the hotel on these dates and go from there. You can go for now."

"That's it? I can go home?"

"For now, but don't go far."

25

KAREN

Day 2 – 21:00
29 hours missing

I collapse onto the couch. The Garda wouldn't tell me anything more as he drove me home from the station. "I know what you know. He arrived in, wouldn't talk to me, but he was very upset."

No news from Fintan in Sligo yet either. I text him.

Fintan, It's Karen. Any update.

He replies almost instantly.

We're on the beach. The Gardai have brought the sniffer dogs in. I will keep you posted.

My phone rings. I have thirty-seven missed calls. Too many to call back, but I pick up when I see Jess's name. "Oh, Jess."

"Karen, I saw the appeal. God love you. I can't even

imagine what you are going through. It's horrendous, beyond horrendous, but I'm calling to say something to you as a friend. You know I love you, and I'll always have your back, but that painting you showed – it's not realistic to think you can find someone from it."

Jess is great but a straight talker. She always shoots from the hip, it's what I love about her usually, but she's wrong in this case. "I know it's the same woman in the CCTV. She has something to do with this."

"And if you keep saying that, Karen, I'm afraid of what people might think." She sighs. "I wish I could be there with you."

"You heard Paddy is in the police station."

"Yeah, it was on the news." Jess worked with both of us, although Paddy and she never liked each other. It made meeting up awkward and, over time, too stressful.

"I have to go do another Facebook Live, then get down to the station."

"Karen, listen to me; listen to what I'm saying."

I hang up, and my phone rings again immediately, the name Michelle Ryan displaying on-screen. I answer. "Karen speaking."

"Karen, it's Michelle Ryan here. I don't know if you remember me. We met at that kid's party in Dublin last year?"

"I remember you, Michelle."

"Oh, Karen, I can't believe what is happening. It's a living nightmare."

I don't have the energy or brain power left to reply.

"I'm sure you're exhausted, so I'll get straight to it. This might sound a bit mad, and I hope it's not insensitive, but Megan was watching your Facebook Live, and in the pictures that Scarlett painted on your wall, there's one with a yellow house and black window frames in the background. Megan thinks she knows the house, and saying that out loud makes me realise how mental I sound."

"Please continue. If Megan is anything like Scarlett, she notices absolutely everything. Scarlett remembers things that had no significance on the day, never mind months later."

"That's exactly it," Michelle says. "I think it's a deaf thing."

I go out to the paintings on the kitchen wall. "Can you describe the house?"

"Yellow with black windows, that's all she said."

There, in the background of one painting is a mustard-coloured house with black window frames. The picture of two girls in swimsuits.

Scarlett and Hope at the beach.

"Did she say where the house is?" I ask.

"Somewhere along the N4, between your house and ours heading west. That's all I have. We're in Sligo, if you remember."

Sligo.

I examine the painting closer. If it's on the N4 west, the closest beach to us is in Sligo.

"I'm sorry I can't be more specific. I keep thinking of Megan if she didn't have her implants. I guess we take them for granted at this point."

"Thanks, Michelle, I am grateful for anything."

"I hope you find her, Karen. I can't even imagine."

I swallow my coffee and take the FM transmitter from its charging cradle where Paddy left it. As I approach my car, a Garda steps out of his marked car into my path. "Going somewhere?"

I don't tell him I'm off to find a house from the background of a painting based on the year-old memory of a child. Hell, it does sound crazy. And yet.

"I'm going to Enniscrone. Fintan said the dogs have arrived."

"If you wait a bit, I'll take you."

"No, I need to go now." There are no cameras, no journalists, and fewer people. "Where's everyone gone?"

"The station. There's another appeal happening any minute." He steps away and rubs his head. "I don't think you should go off by yourself, but I have to stay here. Let me radio for someone to escort you."

"I can't wait around for someone to come. I'll be fine." I don't wait for an answer but drive away, heading for the N4 West. This may be a stab in the dark, but with both Fintan and Michelle singing from the same hymn sheet, I have to check it out. I know what the police will say, and time has surely run out for her batteries; I can't stand by while it runs out for her, too.

I call Paddy and swerve into the path of a lorry, the driver blowing his horn. Using my phone while driving is a bad idea, I above all people should know that. His phone is off. Still in the station. My gut turns. I'm afraid to examine that thought, and I have to concentrate on the landscape as I pass. I slow down, and another lorry sounds its horn. The sun glares in through the windscreen, making it difficult to see, and there are trees obstructing whole sections of the road. I've been driving like this for half an hour, watching houses. It's pointless. I'll take the next slip road and head back home. Then I spot it, in the distance. I pull into the hard shoulder and shade my eyes from the sun, to make sure I'm not dreaming, but I'm not.

A mustard-coloured two-storey house.

THE NEXT EXIT off the N4 doesn't come for ages. I take it, then another left and follow the road back in the direction I came. If I drive parallel to the main road, I should find the house. I don't know this area at all, but it can't be more than twenty kilometres from our house. Yellow fields and rolling hills meeting a thick forest in the distance. The smell of slurry coming in through my car's air conditioning system makes me gag. We always travel east, in the opposite direction of our house. Turn right to Dublin, left to Sligo. Always right. It's where we meet our deaf family friends, or rather acquaintances. When I find Scarlett, I will be present. I will give her life experiences, my attention and focus, everything, on her.

I promise you, Scarlett, I promise.

The road is bumpy but decent. Driving at eighty kilometres per hour, I hit branches and brambles sticking out of the ditches. Taking a corner too hard, I skim the ditch and land on the other side of the road. Thankfully, there are no cars around, so I take a moment to steady myself and drive on. I haven't seen another car since leaving the main road, and I must have been driving ten minutes at this stage. At the top of a small hill, there's a sign on the grass verge to the left.

Failte go Baile an Teann Glann
Welcome to Ballygrave

My Irish is rusty, but I think that translates as "Home of the Graveyard". A strange name. Ballygrave is all of four buildings, it seems – a newsagent's shop, a pub and a community hall attached to a small church. All closed up, like a Wild West town in a theme park. I drive past another sign that says:

Slan abhaile
Safe home

Ahead, four roads meet at a crossroads, none of which have the right of way. There is no sign of the mustard house, so I continue straight through, through the next crossroads and the next. When I find myself back in Ballygrave, I concede I am lost and pull into the pub car park. It will be dark soon, and I can't afford to lose more valuable time driving around in circles.

There's no phone signal, no data (and even if there were, what would I enter into Google Maps?), and not a sinner around to ask for directions. I turn off the car engine. There's no birdsong or cows mooing, and a shiver runs down my spine. This place is deserted. My feet sound too loud on the stony ground. I pull the pub door – it's locked up tight.

The newsagents are closed too, and the other buildings. Still no signal on my phone. I get back into my car and drive away as fast as I can out of this creepy place.

Then I see it. A mustard-coloured house about five hundred metres ahead. I drive on and park up at the top of a hilly driveway leading to an old two-storey farmhouse with an overgrown garden. Dandelions and daisies smatter the front lawn, and the net curtains on the windows are almost brown. The black paint on the front door and window frames is peeling, and I try to call Helen to tell her where I am but still can't get a signal. I sit in the car and watch the house, no sign of life, and try to ring Helen again, hoping against hope to pick up a signal, but after three attempts I drive up to the front door, get out of my car and ring the doorbell.

Nothing.

I cup my hands over my eyes and peer in the window-pane. It looks like old people once lived here; it's dated and neglected. The traffic hums on the N4 in the distance as I ring the doorbell again. Nothing.

I stand there, not knowing what to do, when my phone beeps with a text, which means I have a signal. I get back to my car to call Helen and tell her about this house, but a green cochlear implant appears on-screen.

Right Implant: Connected.
Left implant: Disconnected.

An alert, not a text. The animation of an implant connecting to my phone plays on repeat, which means only one thing: Scarlett is here.

I jump out of the car and ring the doorbell again, and still nobody answers. I lift the letter box. "Hello, can you hear me? Hello?"

A man roars from inside, turning my blood cold. I need to get out of here and call the police. The second I sit in my car, I lock the door, and an involuntary wail leaves my body. I drive down the hill, my legs jelly and black blotches all over my field of vision.

She's here. Scarlett is here. It's not Sligo, but it's on the Sligo road. How did Fintan know? My heart pounds and hands shake as every instinct tells me to go back to the house and rescue her, and it takes every fibre of my being to override it. My head is on fire with permutations and combinations of what is happening to her, but I can't do anything on my own. I need help.

Is she hurting?
What do they want?
How many people are in there?

I'm fingers and thumbs as I swipe my phone: 998... 979... 999. Third time lucky. The "no signal" tone. I drive over the cattle grid and out through the metal gates, turning right when my phone beeps with a different animation on-screen. A yellow and black danger triangle and a cochlear implant with one bar shaded.

Right implant: Low battery.
Left implant: Disconnected.

She still has sound but only through one implant, and that will die any minute. There's no time. If her battery dies, I can't connect to her, and she could be moved, or worse.

I pull to the side of the road, out of view of the house. Fetching the jack from the boot, I go back through the gates, up the hill, keeping tight to the overgrown perimeter hedge and around the back of the house. It's more neglected from this angle, the paint gone completely from one ground-floor windowsill. Apart from the three stone smaller buildings, the yard is deserted.

My phone beeps, startling me and echoing all around.

Right implant: Very low battery.
Left implant: Disconnected.

I hold my breath to see if anybody comes, but the back of the house looms in silence. Where is she? Two of the stone buildings look like old sheds with windows and doors, and the other is a garage of sorts, judging by its wider aluminium door. I don't know what is going to happen next, but Scarlett must be so scared. I have to let her know I am here.

In case I never see her again.

I turn on the FM transmitter and speak into it. "Scarlett, it's Mammy. You can hear me, but I can't hear you. I'm here, and I'm going to get you. You need to be brave. I love you very, very much."

Then I remember, the FM transmitter runs down the battery on the implant.

"I have to go now because you need your battery, but I'm here, and I'm not leaving until I find you."

I power off the FM transmitter and tiptoe to the garage shed, peering in the filthy window. A silver Toyota saloon car is inside the grey concrete room, but it seems otherwise empty. The window on the next building is too dirty to see through, but I turn the wooden handle on the barn-like door, and the latch clicks. Holding my breath, I push it to reveal a grey interior lined with shelves of paint tins, tools, gardening equipment and car accessories under cobwebs, and a rusty green lawnmower is the only thing on the floor.

The third house has windows so dirty I can't see through them again and the same barn-like door. I try the handle, but this one doesn't open. I push against the door, but it doesn't budge.

"Can I help you?"

I turn to see a woman with a shotgun.

26

Day 2 – 22:00

The child colours, then startles, staring into the distance as if listening intently. The light flashes blue on her implant, and she nods before the light flashes green again.

"Who was that?" I ask.

"Nobody."

"I saw the blue light; I know what that means. Who was talking to you?"

"Nobody."

Someone was talking to her.

"I have to go." Upstairs, I glance out the front door, half expecting to see flashing lights and Garda cars everywhere, but there's nothing.

From Daddy's safe in the pantry, I remove his old shotgun when a passing shadow makes me jump, and I paste myself to the wall. Someone walks by the window, just inches from where I stand. I stay deathly still. When the footsteps fade, I peep out the window and can't believe my eyes. It's Karen, and... she appears to be alone.

"Where is she?"

"Keys and phone." A brown-haired woman in shorts and vest points a shotgun at me. Her eyes are wild, but she doesn't falter.

"Who are you?"

"Keys and phone. Now."

I hand them over.

"Walk." She marches me through a small yellow kitchen, into a musty, old hallway and orders me to open the white wooden door ahead. I turn the handle, revealing dark steps descending to a lower level. I hesitate, but she prods me in the shoulder blade with the gun. She is much smaller than me, three or four inches, and wider; I could easily overpower her. If I turn, maybe I could grab—

"Don't try anything funny, or I will kill Scarlett."

"What have you done with her?"

She doesn't answer but switches on the light and prods me down the stairs. A naked bulb illuminates a concrete laundry room that smells of chemicals, and an old tumble dryer and washing machine run. There is another white door ahead.

"Open it," she says.

I consider trying to overpower her again, but her gun is pushed into my back, so I do it, and she pushes me through the doorway. A voice comes from the far corner—

"Mammy?"

"Scarlett!"

She runs at me, and we tumble to the ground, locked in an embrace and crying. I rub her head and cover her face in frantic kisses. "Oh my God. Oh, I've missed you. I love you so much."

"I'm scared, Mammy. I want to go home." She clings to me, sobbing, her implant flashing orange. She's wearing a weird blue dress, like something from an old postcard.

"Scarlett – on the bed," the woman orders.

I hold her tighter.

"Bed. Now." She lifts her gun.

Scarlett pries herself from my arms, still sobbing, and sits up on the bed.

"You, against the wall," she tells me.

I step back. "Who are you?"

She scoffs. "It's tragic that you have to ask me that question. If you were paying the slightest bit of attention to your life, you would know the answer."

I examine her brown eyes bulging in her oval face and her long, dark hair. I have no idea who she is. "You're sick," I say.

She howls laughing, and Scarlett looks terrified.

"That's a good one. Karen O'Hara, the woman who said she wanted her child dead, has the nerve to call me sick. Brilliant!"

She wipes a tear from her eye. Scarlett buries her head into the pillow and cries.

"Scarlett, no. No, I never wanted you dead. She's lying."

"Save it, Karen, she already knows. I showed her the interview."

Shit.

"No, don't believe her, Scarlett," I protest. "I didn't mean it; I love you more than anything."

Scarlett whips around. "You don't love me." She holds my gaze but joins the index and middle finger of her right hand and moves them once from left to right. The sign language for "not". Our secret code for *I am pretending or I don't believe.* My clever little girl.

"I need to do a wee," she says.

The woman nods towards the yellow bucket to my right. "Be my guest."

I go to pass it to Scarlett, but the woman points her gun at me. Scarlett shrieks.

"Don't worry, Scarlett," I say without taking my eyes off the woman, "she wouldn't use the gun, would you?"

She laughs. "Let's not test your theory."

As Scarlett uses the bucket, every bit of me wants to comfort her in this horrible room, cool despite the hot weather outside. She signs "throw," then stands and screams at the top of her voice, throwing the urine at the woman. I lunge, trying to grab the gun, but she is too fast and hits me in the face with the butt of her gun as the urine soaks us both. I stumble in blinding pain.

"Dirty little girl." The woman's eyes darken in her wet face. "Dirty, dirty, dirty."

"The police will find us," I cry. "They saw me leave. They'll come looking."

Scarlett gasps. "Mammy, your face."

Metallic liquid fills my mouth as my left cheek throbs. I wipe it to find it is not urine but blood. "It's okay, honey, it doesn't hurt." My left eye is closing.

"How did you find us?" the woman asks.

"Scarlett painted your house, and I saw it from the main road. Someone will come."

She squeezes the urine from her shorts, and my phone slips from her pocket, through her hands and hits the floor, its screen shattering. When the girls were born, and Hope passed, the messages of support I got carried me through. They were all on my WhatsApp. I didn't want to risk losing them in a change of phone, so I kept this one, the one that now lies in pieces on the concrete floor. I can't let her see my pain.

"My husband will find me. My car is parked outside for a start."

She laughs hard. "Your husband, you mean my lover, Paddy? The one who was leaving you for me?"

My stomach flips. "No, he wouldn't."

The woman takes out another phone, all the while holding the gun.

"Oh, he would. Paddy would. Paddy would many, many times." She taps and shows me the screen. Paddy in bed with her.

"You? And Paddy? Who *are* you?"

"I wanted to do this" – she waves the gun at us – "the easy way. I gave him a chance to find his balls, to leave you, but he chickened out at the last hurdle. He wanted to have it both ways – me and Scarlett. So here we are."

"How long has it been going on?"

She smirks. "Months."

I knew it. "So that's what this is? You stole my daughter to get back at my husband? You're deranged."

She laughs. "Oh my God, you still don't get it, do you? This was NEVER about your husband. I mean, I was willing to put up with him if it meant helping – loving – a child, but that was all. This was always about Scarlett."

"Why? Why my daughter? You don't even know her."

"Correction. It's *you* who doesn't know her. Scarlett's a wonderful child if you'd bother to look up from your phone once in a while; you'd see she's a child who was almost taken, but you didn't even realise that, did you, Karen?"

"I know she's wonderful. She's the best thing I've ever... hold on, what did you say?"

"Yes. That's right. Remember the day in Belvedere when you found her by the lake on her own? Did you know she was approached by a middle-aged man? Of course you didn't. You were more worried about your coffee than your daughter, and God only knows what would have happened if I weren't there to protect her. I can't leave her with you. She needs me."

I remember the day, but she was only gone for a minute, wasn't she? "You're crazy."

"Scarlett, tell your mother who I am."

"Hope," Scarlett says, and the woman grins.

"I knew it. But Hope in the pictures has blonde hair and... a wig? You disguised yourself."

She kneels beside me. "Oh, it must feel awful, your child told you all about me, drew me and my house, but you didn't ever see me. I've been watching you both for a very long time now."

I shudder. "Scarlett told me she was going to the beach with you, but this is nowhere near the beach."

She laughs again. "That is what is known as a bum steer, my dear. In case you finally started to listen."

28

Day 2 – 22:30

The Gardai issued a Section 10 of the criminal justice miscellaneous provisions act warrant and searched the house, car and office. They've taken my phone and laptop too, and two of them sit outside our house in a marked car. More Gardai hold back the crowd, increasing by the minute. I'm under surveillance, that's what they said, but I don't care about any of that. I desperately need Scarlett home.

Karen is on her way to Enniscrone to meet Fintan; they told me I'm not allowed to follow. Scarlett's room has been upended, her clothes and toys strewn across the floor. I pick up Henry, her polar bear soft toy with the cochlear implants, off the floor and hug it, remembering the day she got it. The surgery to implant both ears was a massive decision, and handing her over to strangers to be operated on terrifying, but Karen and I were united in our belief that it was the right thing to do. Then followed the longest wait while both ears healed until, a month later, her implants were activated and switched on. At sixteen months old, she heard again for the first time since she lost her hearing at a few days old. The sheer joy when she reacted to sound was mind-blowing, both of us feeling as if we had witnessed a miracle. That day I asked Karen to marry me, and she said yes.

Back in the empty office, the photo taken days after Scarlett's activation hangs on the wall, the three of us beaming at the camera. The PC whirrs as the monitor power button blinks green. I press enter, and the screen lights up with Karen's Facebook page open. One hundred and three messages and two hundred and thirty-six notifications.

I begin to click through them, one by one.

Hi Karen, I think I saw your little girl in Belfast. She was in a van with two men.

Saying prayers for her safe return.

You get what you wish for.

I grab a notepad and pen and begin to write all the leads down, no matter how small. A message pops up in the bottom right of the screen.

Hello Karen, my name is Ciara Turner. I have been following your daughter's case from the UK. Please give me a call. I have information that might help.

I call the number on-screen, and it is answered on the first ring.

"Ciara Turner." A woman with an Irish accent.

"Hello, Ciara. It's Paddy O'Hara, Scarlett's father. You sent my wife, Karen, a message through Facebook?"

"Oh, Paddy, that's right. Yes, I did." A glass smashes on the other end. I didn't check the time she sent the message; it could have been hours ago. However, drunk now is better than sober too late.

"Any update on Scarlett?" she asks.

I swallow. "Not yet. You have information, you say?"

"It might not be connected, but I thought you should know. I'd want to know if it was my child missing. Two years ago, my daughter Lucy was abducted from nursery."

"That's really terrible; sorry to hear that."

"Yes. Terrible indeed. A woman who worked there took her. We thought she loved Lucy, and she did. The problem was, she loved her too much."

"What happened?"

"She took her one day. Out of the nursery. Off in her car."

"Did your daughter... Was she okay?"

"Oh yes, unharmed physically, but who knows what would have happened if the nursery staff hadn't realised and alerted the police. I know what you are going through; it is the worst thing a parent can experience."

"What happened your daughter?"

"It was Lucy's last day in that nursery. We were moving her because that woman had become fixated on Lucy. We should have moved her much, much earlier in hindsight, but life was busy, and we ignored the signs until it was too late. She begged us not to press charges, and I guess a parent's guilt... Anyway, in the end we did press charges. She did the whole 'poor me' act to perfection. She was like a different person, it was scary, and the judge almost apologised in handing her a suspended sentence. It was in the news at the time. I still feel guilty."

I can relate to it all. "It wasn't your fault."

She scoffs. "It wasn't *not* our fault. We'd started a business and were chasing some big contracts. We should have paid more attention to what was happening with Lucy, moved her out of that nursery sooner. I'd noticed some funky behaviour from that woman, but it was a busy time in work, and we took our eye off the ball. In court, she claimed she was taking Lucy to the beach as a parting gift because she'd never been, and she was right. That was a bitter pill to swallow."

A bead of sweat runs down the back of my neck. "That doesn't excuse what she did."

"Hmm. Thankfully Lucy wasn't harmed, but I often wonder about that woman. I mean, that's not right, taking a child, regardless of her motivation."

"It's not right at all. Were you in the UK at the time, Ciara?"

"Yes, we were. London, but this woman was Irish."

I fall into the office chair as she continues. "She was Irish, this woman with a strong midlands accent. Not unlike mine, I'm originally from Offaly myself. She moved away from our area shortly after the court case; she could have gone home. Google her; the reports are still online. You'll see who she is. Elaine Murtagh."

"Thank you, Ciara," I say, mad to run a search. "I'll go do that now."

"I hope you find her."

I search for the words "Elaine Murtagh London child," and a rake of articles fills my screen, including:

Toddler abducted from local nursery.

Trial of the childcare worker Elaine Murtagh starts today.

Suspended sentence for childcare worker.

I open the first article and cannot believe the picture that is displayed before my eyes.

It's Rose.

29

Two years ago

Every morning she arrives to the nursery in her Audi. Ciara Turner. Elegant and sharp, her tailored suits screaming money. She takes her designer baby chair from her new 4x4 while holding her mobile phone under her made-up chin.

"No outside footwear," the sign in the baby room says. Most parents interpret this as a directive to remove their shoes or to cover them in the disposable blue anti-static covers left in the box at the door while they try to part themselves from their children.

Not Ciara Turner. She seems to think it means:

Stand outside the door, call a member of staff and hand the baby in from the door. While still talking on the phone.

Every morning she hands over her precious baby to me, still in her sleepsuit with a sodden heavy nappy from the night before. Lucy's huge smile and outstretched arms when she sees me say it all. She adores coming here. She adores me.

My colleagues are adequate but young, more concerned with their weekend plans and their cigarette breaks than their tiny charges. This isn't the chosen career for many of them, but a stopgap on their way to figure out who they are.

For me, children are my passion, my world, even before I knew I would never be a mother. When I applied to become a foster carer back in Ireland, it was an emphatic no. My mental health and self-harm records meant I was incompatible with the position, allegedly, yet who would know better what an abused or neglected child would need? However, working with them in a nursery didn't cause an issue.

Ever since I was a teen, children have been the sunshine in my life. You wouldn't have to be a genius to make the link between that and my mother dying when I was young. That is no doubt what the outside world think, and they're right to a degree, but babysitting offered my first chance to get away from him. The children were a bonus.

When they took my womb and ovaries, I thought life was over, but coming to London saved me. A change of scenery in this cosmopolitan city, I can be anyone I want here or nobody at all. Working Monday to Friday in the nursery fills my days, and although weekends are long, life is bearable. I've made my peace with never hearing the word mama, so when Lucy Turner grew to a toddler and called me that beautiful word, I was overjoyed. With chestnut eyes and long black lashes, she is the highlight of my day. I ache for her every weekend, and while most people hate them, I live for Monday mornings. She's always the first child in to the nursery in the morning and last out in the evening. I volunteer regularly for overtime, which pleases Jill, the manager of the centre, and staff alike, delighted they don't have to do it. Sometimes, in my one-bed flat, I can barely sleep thinking of Lucy, wondering if her parents have any idea how amazing she is. I'm utterly content in her company, happy to provide her with the unconditional love she doesn't get at home.

One Thursday, I dash into town on my lunch break to pick up Christmas presents for Lucy. I'm always buying her little things and hiding them amongst the nursery toys. Besides, I have nobody else to buy for. The atmosphere is festive, the cold air coloured by the lights, and I hum along with the carol singers as I stroll along Kensington High Street. Life is good.

Delighted with my purchases – I'd found all her favourite things – spotting the book in the shop window made my day.

As I pass the Ivy Kensington Brasserie, I spy the Turners, Lucy's parents, at a window table. I should keep going, but seeing them laughing and quaffing wine while Lucy is in the nursery, as she has been every open moment this week, is too much to take.

I steel myself and enter the restaurant. Ciara's face drops when she sees me. Good! I want her to know I saw her. I want her to be ashamed. She isn't unlike me, our accents are similar, yet she thinks her shit doesn't stink like mine. The only difference between me and her is she was born to a different family. As I approach, she recovers and paints on a smile.

"Hello Elaaaaaiiine, what a surprise!" Her words are slow and pronounced, the midlands accent fading with every passing day we meet. "Having a long liquid lunch."

I shrug.

"We deserve it, right, darling?" She clinks her wine glass against her husband's – Giles, a high-end attorney.

"Ciara won the Callaghan contract. You know the Callaghan family, the actors?" he asks.

Everyone knows them. *The Waltons* meet *Little House on the Prairie*. Traditionalists, albeit multimillionaire traditionalists.

She crosses her long, lean black trouser-suited legs. "It

will mean I have to put in more hours at the office, but it's a huge deal."

I take the hardbacked book from my tote bag and run my hand over the sky-blue cover. *A Day at the Beach* by Lucy Kelvin. "I bought this for Lucy; it's her favourite book in the nursery. She's so adorable and clever. Do you know she underlines the name Lucy with her finger and points to her chest? She was so distraught when one of our toddlers had an accident on it and it was binned. I've been trying to get another copy but had no luck until now. She's going to be ecstatic."

I don't mention all the other gifts in my bag are for Lucy too. I pass the book to Ciara. "She loves reading it, in the nursery, with me. So clever."

She looks at her husband, not the book, and clears her throat. "About that... we've been meaning to talk to you. You have been marvellous, but we have found a new nursery for Lucy."

My head swims, my legs wobble, and I hold on to a table to stop myself falling. "What? When?"

"After Christmas. This is her last week in the nursery." She clicks her fingers and calls for the bill.

"No. No, you can't take her. Why?"

When a waiter brings the bill, we fall silent, and he leaves the tense scene. "The new nursery is closer to our home and—"

"Tell the girl the truth," Giles says, placing his credit card into the leather bill holder. The waiter returns with the card machine. This time I don't quieten.

"What truth? Ciara, what is he talking about?"

Ciara brushes a lock of black hair behind her ear to reveal diamond clusters. "We, Giles and I, feel your connection with Lucy is, how shall I put it?"

"Creepy," he says, and the waiter's eyes dart to the floor.

"Intense," she says, glaring at her husband. "We've spoken to Jill, and she understands. We didn't mention you, we felt that would be unfair, but it's healthier all round for us to find another place for Lucy."

They don't understand. "Please don't. She needs me."

Ciara stands, placing her fur coat around her shoulders. "It is done." As she passes me, I grab her arm, but she yanks it back, knocking my bag and its contents all over the restaurant floor. Her mouth falls open as she surveys all the presents on display; then she shakes her head and continues walking.

I run after her. "Maybe I could visit at the weekend. I'll take Lucy out; give you guys a break. You work hard."

She whips around, eyes narrowed. "Let me be clear. You are so far past appropriate. This obsession with our daughter is worrying. We believe for everyone involved it is best if she moves away and your association with her stops."

Giles opens the restaurant door. "Where to first, darling?" he asks his wife as if nothing has happened. As if my world hasn't just ended.

She pulls her fur coat tight around her and steps out into the cold day. "Maybe Harvey Nichols?"

Back in the nursery, I sit on a play mat, dazed and confused, while the toddlers play around me. Lucy toddles over and peers into my shopping bag, squealing with delight when she spots the book. She pulls it from the bag and hugs me hard. I take it to the rocking chair, where she climbs onto my knee and snuggles in while I read to her, tears streaming down my face. Her warm breath slows and deepens, her little dimpled hand twirling my hair. This is all wrong. She needs me as much as I need her.

I glance outside the glass windows into the baby room, where two of my young colleagues discuss the weekend ahead and babies cry or kick toys hanging from play mats.

The others must have taken an extended lunch break. Jill is absent today.

"I'm putting this one down for a sleep," I say. They barely acknowledge me as I carry the drowsy child past their room, out through reception, past the room filled with cots, and straight out the front door, taking a blanket and car seat from inside the door as I leave.

With trembling hands and a thumping heart, I strap her into my red Fiat Punto and drive out of the crèche in the direction of the coast.

I only have her for a few hours; I have to show her the beach. She's never been, and that breaks my heart. My lovely mother would have given anything to stay with me.

I switch on the radio, and "Last Christmas" plays through the speakers as she drifts off to sleep. I keep driving, determined to get to the ocean, and soon I'm out of city traffic and heading for the coast.

"Mama?" Lucy is awake. She sits up, trying to see out her window.

"Hello, sleepyhead!"

She giggles. "Sheepy head."

"Lucy, honey, we are going to the seaside."

She squeals and claps her hands. "She. Hurray. She."

I put my foot down on the accelerator. They have surely noticed her gone at this stage; all hell is breaking loose in the nursery no doubt. They'll call the police, which will mean a lot of trouble for me, but that's not my concern. I have to get her to the seaside. I promised I would bring her, and I intend to keep that promise. Together we sing "The wheels on the Bus" as I try to absorb every minute. There is nothing, and I am nothing without her.

"Lucy, this is our last day together." I pass the book to her in the back seat. "I want you to remember how much you are loved when you read this book."

She bats the book away with her little hand. "No, Mama, want you."

I consider the life ahead for her. An absent mother and a father who is no better. How can I leave her to this life? A child with nobody to care for her. A vulnerable child who will never know how it feels to be loved. I can't stand by and watch any child grow up like I did, least of all my beautiful Lucy. Maybe I should keep driving, all the way to France. I don't notice the sirens or the flashing lights calling to pull over until I turn onto a bridge ahead, and it is blocked with police cars. Behind me, two cars block me in. There is only one way out, and that is over the edge, into the deep water. For a minute I consider, but it is a minute too long. Lucy screams as I am pulled out of the car by the neck. "No, Mama, no," she cries, reaching for me as they carry her off, and I am handcuffed over the seawater that laps beneath us.

I spend the next day in the police station, sticking to the story that I was taking the child for a goodbye drive along the seafront, fully intending to return her. The Turners press charges regardless.

That was the last time I spoke to Lucy or held her in my arms, but I monitor her from a distance. Life for Lucy has worsened. Instead of 7am to 6pm five days a week, she attends her new nursery from 7am to 7pm six days per week. On Sundays, when they take her out, she shuffles along like a zombie. I want to tell them her favourite food is pasta shells in tomato sauce with broccoli, and her favourite song is "Ring a Ring o' Roses," but I can't. I consider sending the book, but then they'd know.

I'm lucky to get a suspended sentence, my solicitor says. It's traumatic to have my face all over the news, and I hate being the centre of attention, all eyes on me, but this too shall pass. It's not long after that Daddy gets sick, and I come home to mind him, which gives me a chance to escape and space to think.

I let Lucy down. My first mistake was showing the strength of my feelings. I should have curbed my enthusiasm, played the long game. Secondly, when I had her in my car, I should never have let her go back to that life. I should have driven straight off that bridge. The next time I won't be so stupid, and as luck would have it, the next time presents itself soon after when Karen O'Hara appears on national TV. I monitor from a distance, but when Scarlett is in danger, the plan changes. It's no longer enough to watch. I must act.

Nine months ago

I WATCH him from the pub across the road for weeks. He's nothing to write home about and certainly not my type. Every Monday, Tuesday and Friday the same routine. Lunch break at 12:35pm exactly in the same cafe. In time, I progress to the cafe and observe him ordering ham salad on granary and an Americano to take away. Every time the same. There's no light in his eyes, and although well dressed, he seems... pathetic.

After a few weeks, dressed in a navy dress, jacket and court shoes, I wait behind him in the café queue. Two young women chat at a nearby table in pink overalls and runners. You don't need to check their name badges to know they're childcare workers, and my heart hurts. When they go to leave, I catch a glimpse of one of their name tags. Rose Hayes, Exception-L. Young, jovial and going back to a job I would love; what I would give to be Rose Hayes.

"Would you like to go ahead?" he asks, looking through me. "I'm waiting for a sandwich."

Hiding in plain sight means becoming the object of the other person's desires. A chameleon. I know what this man needs. I put my hand on his forearm, and he jolts. Now I have his attention. "Thank you, you are so kind. I was going to order a sandwich myself. What would you recommend?" I hold his gaze for five, then look away, like I practised.

He tilts his head and regards me with an expression of curiosity. "I usually get the ham salad, it's good."

I order the sandwich as recommended. "Lovely day out there," I say to him as the deli assistant prepares it. "Do you work around here?"

"Close by. You?"

"Exception-L. I manage the childcare facility there." This is thrilling.

"Sounds great. Sorry, do I know you?"

I run my fingers through my straightened hair and laugh. "Not that I know of, but someone who offers their place in the queue deserves a kindness, wouldn't you think?"

Is he blushing? "Um... I suppose..."

"Rose. Rose Hayes." I hold out my hand, which he accepts and shakes with a soft hand. I can't tell him my real name; the game will be up before it begins. Then my sandwich is ready, and I pay, leave and go home.

A week later we "accidentally" meet again.

"We must stop meeting like this," I say in the queue, and this time he definitely blushes. "You know my name, but I don't know yours."

"Paddy. Paddy O'Hara, and you are Rose, right?"

A table beside us vacates. "I have a longer break today and was planning on sitting in today." I gesture to the empty table. "Care to join me?"

His eyes dart around the café as if checking for someone, and his shoulders slump. "I'd best get back to work."

"No problem. Another time?" I flutter my eyelashes.

His eyes darken. "Another time."

I don't go the following week, but the next week when I walk through the door, he is already sitting at a table, and his face lights up. That's it. A weekly, then biweekly lunch date that quickly turns physical. Hotels and the car park in his office, I always pay from my ample savings. Despite all his talk of what a big job he has, and blaming a paper trail for not paying his way, the tight git is only too happy to let me pay, which I do in cash. Upset with his wife, taken with his daughter, obsessed with his job and so very easy to manipulate, we have so much in common. Well, the created version of me. I have a whole fake life made up ready for when he asks, but he rarely does. I am simply there to make him feel good. It's a match made in heaven. He hates social media, which is music to my ears, and when he mentions they're thinking about moving house a month into our relationship, it is easy to sway his decision on where to go. It's like taking candy from a baby he is such a pushover, and sometimes I feel bad, but all is fair in love and war, and these are the sacrifices women make for children, like my mother made for me.

30

KAREN

Day 2 – 23:30

"Who are you?" My face pulsates.

She smirks. "Call me Hope."

"Never. What are you going to do with us? You can't keep us here indefinitely; the whole country is looking for Scarlett and soon will be looking for me too."

"Shut up."

"We can't be far from our house as the crow flies. The jig's up. Let us go while you can."

"Shut up. Shut up. Shut up! Let me think."

I sign "sign" to Scarlett.

She gazes at a point just past me.

I sign "man upstairs?"

She signs back "her daddy – sick."

The woman's eyes dart from Scarlett to me and back again. "What are you two saying?" Her agitation grows.

I soften my voice. "I'll drive you wherever you want to go. Start afresh, put all this behind you."

She laughs. "You must think I'm an idiot."

"I don't. I think you're a good person whom Paddy used. He led you to think he would leave me and that you could be a family. All of this isn't your fault, it's his."

"Scarlett, come over here."

"My battery is dead." She takes the implant off her right ear; the light's gone out.

"Put the other one on," the woman says and gestures at the other implant on the table.

Scarlett swaps them around, and the light turns green on her left ear. "I can hear you now."

"Come here, Scarlett," she says, and Scarlett shakes her head. The woman lunges, grabbing her, and jams the barrel of the gun into her arm. Scarlett whimpers. She throws a key at me. "Open the door."

I unlock the door, and the three of us move through the darkness of the basement, up the stairs and into the main house. It is dark outside. The moans coming from upstairs turn my stomach, and the stench is foul. She doesn't switch the light on as we make our way through the house.

"Your daddy is sad," Scarlett says as we pass the foot of the stairs.

"Keep walking," the woman commands. He cries out long and loud.

"Please help him," Scarlett begs.

"He's a bad man; he doesn't deserve help, trust me."

31

ELAINE

Daddy's crying turns to a gurgling and then stops. A shiver runs through me, but I don't go to him. He doesn't deserve my sympathy.

He's despicable. Everybody turned a blind eye to me: a small child, sleeping every night on my mother's grave, nodding off in school, telling the truth in confession and being thrown out for my dirty mouth. It wasn't my fault the language I had was what he gave me. No wonder I upped and left as soon as I could.

He never looked for me. Never. When I came home to bury Emily, I told him to stay away. I wanted her buried with Mammy. Then Father Kelly tracked me down and asked me to come home from England to mind Daddy. The mere thought of being in his company repulsed me, but after the incident with Lucy, I needed somewhere to retreat to, and Ballygrave was the perfect haven.

"Where are you taking us?" Karen asks.

I pull Scarlett to me, and she squeals. "You'll drive. Don't think of trying anything, or I'll blow her head off."

Scarlett's implant flashes green in the clear night as we walk in silence to Karen's car parked on the road outside. I throw her the keys, and she fidgets before opening the car door.

Scarlett trembles and yanks her wrist. "Ow, that hurts."

I loosen my grip but push the gun into her back. Karen sits in the car and starts the engine, her full beams lighting up the road.

"Turn off the lights!"

She obeys, and I open the back door of the car, throwing the child onto the back seat. She squeals, and her mother glances behind through the rear-view mirror. The look between the child and her mother brings me back to the time when he would throw me to the ground and my mother would stand in front of me, helpless and begging him not to hurt me. The futility, the hopelessness, the not being able to save each other.

Too late, I notice Karen's hands are moving in shapes. She screams, "Now," and Scarlett dives across the back seat, the car speeding off. I pull the trigger, the shot ringing out into the night. The car skids across the road and plunges into the forest.

I run to them; the child's screams guiding me. Enabling the torch on my phone, I see her in the front seat, holding her mother's head. Blood is seeping from Karen's shoulder onto Scarlett's dress. My blue dress, the one I wore for Mammy's funeral.

"Mammy, please wake up. Please."

She spits at me. "She's dead! You killed my mammy. I hate you."

I stumble back. What have I done? All I wanted was to protect and love a child, but I've killed her mother in front of her. The Gardai will find her, they'll find her, and I'll go to prison. I don't care about me; Scarlett is my only concern. Without me, she'll grow up without a mother to protect her, vulnerable like me. I can't let that happen to her; I'm not a monster. "Sweetie, it's too late; let's go."

"What?"

"It's too late. Leave her."

She cradles her mother, in floods of tears.

I don't want to but have no choice. I nudge her with the gun. "Let's go."

"I hate you," she screams.

I walk her further into the dark woods, using the torch to light our way. Her implant flashes ahead as she sobs. That battery will die soon, not that it matters anymore. Everything I touch turns bad.

We reach the edge of the woods, and the graveyard comes into view under the clear night sky.

She stiffens. "Where are you bringing me?"

"To visit my family."

"But... they're dead."

"There is nothing to be frightened of with the dead; it is the living we should be scared of."

Past the uneven graves, we stop at Mammy's grave and kneel down. I yank Scarlett onto her knees beside me, and she yelps as she hits the ground. A spider scuttles across the small white cross beside Mammy's.

Emily Murtagh
Six hours old
Angel

In the distance, a wailing siren and flashing lights herald the passing of a Garda car on the N4 towards Sligo. Then another and another. I stand and strain to see if they take the turn for Ballygrave when an excruciating pain runs through my hand. I pull it away, deep pools of blood forming in my palm. I've been bitten.

She scarpers as quick as lightning. I lunge to stop her, grabbing her ankle, but she kicks hard and clambers to her feet, speeding through the graveyard gates. I follow, but she is too agile for me, twisting and turning, and then she disappears into the black woods. Now I can take my time.

The woods are my playground; I know every inch of them. A childhood spent hiding from Daddy, they were my haven. I stand still, listening for the snap of a branch, the flight of a bird, anything that will tell me where she is. There is nothing. No sound. I turn off the light on my phone.

She will never find her way out of these woods. The briars, dips and drops are difficult in the daytime for the unfamiliar trekker, but at night she has no chance. Deeper in the woods, the trees have blocked out all light, but I know them well. I stop in the centre and listen. Nothing.

"Scarlett, I'm not going to hurt you. I love you. Come out, come out, wherever you are."

And then I see it in the distance. Faint but there – a flashing orange light.

"Ah, there you are," I say. The light is no longer green, which means her battery is dying. It could go out at any second, and then she'll get away, back to what? A miserable life thanks to me? I can't let that happen; I let Lucy down, I won't do it again. With shallow breath, I approach the flashing light and raise my gun.

Please, Mammy, look after her for me.

I pull the trigger, and the shot rings out all around, the woods lighting up momentarily. There is nobody there. I enable my torch, which illuminates the area, revealing the implant sitting on a bush. The light stops flashing.

She can't have got far. She has no hearing, and the woods

are pitch black. She'll trip, she'll stumble, she'll – but there is no sound. She can't have made her way back. Nobody could find their way out of here without knowing the woods. I put myself in her shoes. If I were eight years old, what would I do?

32

My head throbs. I attempt to move, but everything spins, and my neck explodes in pain. I'm in a car, and my shoulder is drenched. I touch it and flinch from the pain. The liquid is blood, and it's mine.

Scarlett!

A shot rings out from the woods. Scarlett. I have to get to her. I pull myself out of the car but only get a few steps before I break out in a sweat and fall. My head is light, and I am losing a lot of blood, but I drag myself along the ground when I hear footsteps. Someone is coming. I reach out but grasp a rose bush, the thorns puncturing my skin, the pain electrifying me, but screaming is not an option. I hold my breath, the pain searing through my arm.

The running stops beside me. It is pitch black, and I fade in and out of consciousness but force my hand onto the thorny rose bush to keep conscious. Then a whisper.

"Mammy?"

"Scarlett, over here."

"Mammy? I can't hear you, and I can't see you, but I remember you're here."

In excruciating pain, I pull myself along the ground until I feel her ankle. She dives down on me, hugging the shoulder that was shot. I pass out.

"Get up, Mammy. Please get up." I open my eyes, but it's too black to see. Scarlett is trying to drag me by the feet. I moan with the pain as a jagged branch rips the skin on my back, but she keeps pulling me along the ground. There is no light on her ears, she can't hear me, and it's too dark for her to see me.

Sirens wail in the distance. Maybe they are coming for us. If Scarlett could get out onto the road and wave them down, we might survive this, but I can't communicate to her, and she continues to drag me, but I am too heavy, and she drops my legs. A twig snaps on the ground to my right. Then a moment later, another one, this time closer.

"Who's there?" I cry.

There is no reply, but another twig snaps.

"Do what you want to me, but let Scarlett go. Please don't hurt her. Don't hurt my baby."

No reply again. Scarlett falls on top of me and whispers, "Sorry, Mammy, I can't carry you."

I pull her hand to me, and outline the letters *r*, *u* and *n* on her palm.

"I don't understand," she cries.

I do it again. *R*, *u* and *n*, but she just lies on me, sobbing, and as I drift away, another shot pierces the air.

33

ELAINE

Scarlett is exactly where I expected, at the entrance to the woods, dragging something along the ground in the darkness. Her mother. As the child grunts and pants, the hopelessness of the situation kills me. I've done this to her.

Why did Karen have to come here? Why couldn't she have just let us be? I only ever wanted to save Scarlett, to show her unconditional love and attention, but now I know. It was never possible; the sacred bond between mother and child should never be broken.

I know; I had it with Mammy. And Emily.

Scarlett grunts and drags in the darkness. I can't let her grow up without a mother like I did. I love her too much. Just like a dog must be put down when in pain, I have to be brave. She doesn't deserve the life ahead of her without her mother; she doesn't deserve to know hardships like I did. In the darkness, I cock the gun and raise it.

Go be with your mother.

"Who's there?"

Karen?

I freeze.

"Do what you want to me, but let Scarlett go. Please don't hurt her. Don't hurt my baby."

She's alive? Scarlett flops onto her mother, and I'm a child again, hugging a Mammy so sick she couldn't open her eyes, and my heart breaks. I miss her so much. Reading to her as she declined, not aware that her end was already written. Then I'm a mother, holding my silent baby. The same story all over again, destined to repeat. Or is it?

I run back through the woods; the sirens tell me the police are coming. A branch gashes my leg, but I feel no pain. I imagine Mammy holding Emily, hand outstretched, beckoning me home. At the top of the hill, the sky full of stars is magical. I lie on Mammy's grave one last time and pull the trigger.

34

KAREN

The next day

I try to open my eyes. It's too bright. I lift my hand to shade my eyes, but it stings. There is something in it, a needle, I think, yes, a needle with a tube leading from it. I follow the tube with my fingers, but a wave of exhaustion washes over me. I'll close my eyes for a minute.

I wake again. Someone is holding my hand. I force my eyes open to see my mother. "Mam?"

"Oh, Karen." She kisses my hand and cries for the second time in my life. "How are you? Are you in pain?"

The room is tiny, but filled with bouquets, soft toys and cards. I don't need to ask where I am this time, the pain shooting through my shoulder as I move providing the answer. I remember with a jolt. The gunshot.

"Scarlett? Where's Scarlett? Is she okay?"

My mother rubs my hand, her face pained.

"Oh no. Please, no..."

"She's having lunch in the canteen. I'll get her."

I let the tears flow, this time with happiness. She's okay.

Scarlett is okay. Things will change from here. No more distractions, no more being a passenger in my own life. My mother returns with Scarlett, who runs and throws herself full force onto the bed. "Mammy!"

"Easy, Scarlett, watch your mother's shoulder."

"I'm so happy to see you, monkey." I rub her hair, feeling her softness and inhaling her freshly washed scent. Her cochlear implants flash green.

"This little lady is so clever. Do you know she tricked that woman with her implants and found her way through the woods in the dark with no sound?"

"I can tell her myself, Granny," Scarlett says and clears her throat. "I put my implant on a bush to trick her and ran back to you. I wasn't as scared of the dark as when I thought you were dead."

A nurse enters with a dishevelled Paddy in tow. Wearing jeans and a navy hoodie, his unshaven face grey. He takes one look at me and bursts into tears.

"No, Paddy, not this time."

He steps back. "I'm so sorry. I've been a fool."

Scarlett looks from me to him, and my mother says, "Scarlett, why don't we go to the shop and get Mammy an ice cream?"

"I want to stay – fine!"

She shuts the door behind them, and Paddy sits on the corner of the bed. "What happened?" I ask.

"I discovered who Rose, I mean Elaine, was. The Gardai found where she lived and came straight away. Scarlett saw the flashing lights of the Garda cars and led them to you. You were passed out when they arrived. I'm so sorry."

"Save it, Paddy. I'm done with you."

He looks to the floor. "You're going to take Scarlett."

"I don't want you here; please leave." I turn away from him.

He lingers in the doorway. "I really am sorry."

"What was it, Paddy, what was it that she had that I didn't?"

"She made me feel special. I was never good enough for you."

I turn to face him, tears streaming down his face.

"You were. You just didn't see it. Anyway, you are welcome to each other."

He wipes his cheek. "She's gone now; she won't be bothering us again."

The gunshot.

"What happened to her?"

"She took her own life. They found her on her mother's grave and her father dead in his bed."

"I hope you're proud of yourself. You messed up her head."

"No, that was done a long time before I came along. She wasn't well at all. She tried this before and pretended to me she was someone else entirely."

"Who was she?"

"Her name was Elaine Murtagh, but she told me her name was Rose. It wasn't the only thing she lied about."

"Goodbye, Paddy. Have your stuff gone from the house by the time I get back."

He doubles back. "Wait. You're not moving to Portugal? But your mother said she's taking you two back with her. I didn't object. I didn't think I had the right to in the circumstances, but obviously I don't want you to take Scarlett away."

I sigh. "Paddy, have you ever listened to me? I mean really listened to me? I would never take her from you. I always wanted a dad to love, and she has one. Sure, you could have been around more, but why would I take her away from you?"

"She really is the best thing I've ever done."

I think back to the day I met her, that tiny baby in the incubator, and my fears that she might never hear birdsong, talk, hear music or say the word "Mama". I think of the clever, chatty little girl who found her way through the woods, told us so much through her paintings when we wouldn't listen, tricked Elaine with her implants and managed to stay alive. "The best thing I've ever done too."

He rubs his eyes. "I wish we'd communicated better."

"You and me both."

"Maybe we could try again?"

"Goodbye, Paddy."

EPILOGUE
KAREN

Three months later

The rescheduled "Fairy Tales: A Theory of Mind over Matter" seminar is a sell-out success.

Dressed in a royal blue shift dress and navy court shoes, the grey-haired Dr Goldberg beams from the stage. "Thank you all for your attendance and attention. I hope you found today's seminar informative and worth the wait. I love you, Ireland!"

The City Conference Centre pulled out all the stops, and the Dromod Hotel changed the doctor's booking without a quibble. The whole cost of her visit is more than covered by today's ticket sales.

She hushes the crowd. "It takes guts, organisation and determination to bring an event of this size to fruition. Like language development, this takes a lot of work and often happens behind the scenes. Can you put your hands together for the woman who made today's seminar possible, and my new business manager, Ms. Karen Sullivan!"

I squeeze Scarlett, who claps beside me along with the enthusiastic audience. Paddy dropped her home on Sunday after her weekend in Granny Elenora's house, where he is back living, laden down with gifts. His mother made contact once she heard we'd split. Scarlett says Granny insists on calling her Elenora, but she doesn't mind because she knows that's not her real name, but it makes Granny happy.

With my hair swept into a bun, and dressed in a fitted black trouser suit with silk white vest, I step onto the stage.

"Speech," someone shouts from the audience, and Dr Goldberg extends her hand towards the podium. I accept, taking my place behind the microphone. Every eye in the packed room looks to me. I am ready for this.

"It is an honour to host Dr Goldberg and a pleasure to organise this conference. Listening to her today and implementing her strategies will help your children so much, you don't realise how much. Fairy tales are fertile ground, they teach our children to think outside the box, and they can teach us some things too."

There is a ripple of laughter. "Thank you, Dr Goldberg, for this opportunity, I look forward to working with you – virtually of course." I clap for her, and the audience joins in. I wait until they quieten down, and take a deep breath.

"I'd like to divert for a minute and address the elephant in the room. You would have to be living under a rock not to know what my family has been through; something I hope you never have to experience first-hand. Thank you for all the support; it means so much. I stand here in front of you, a mother and a woman who, just over a year ago, was cancelled over an ill-chosen word. A woman who made and will continue to make mistakes. We teach our children to forgive but forget to listen ourselves. If you are judging people by their actions, online or otherwise, remember they are human beings who make mistakes just like you and I. Be kind."

The audience jump to their feet, clapping and cheering.

"Oh, and just one more thing. I used to think giving up your seat was essential to be a good parent, but it's not. There are enough seats for us all. Thank you."

ACKNOWLEDGMENTS

This book would not exist without a cast of thousands. Here are but a few, apologies to those I have forgotten. There will be at least one, there always is.

The amazing team at Inkubator Books, especially to Brian Lynch. Your level of support, time and direction was unexpected; this book would not exist without you.

Kate Gallagher and Alice Latchford for your story edits, Shirley Khan for the copy edit, and Pauline Nolet for the proofread.

John Quinn and Brian Willoughby. Initially contacted with police procedural questions, your help and encouragement went above and beyond. All mistakes are entirely my own.

Seamus Sheridan, for your firearm knowledge.

Amie Healy Connor and Maureen Delaney for your medical knowledge.

Early readers: Rachel Broderick, Aisling Cahill, Tracey Dunlop, Laura Keating Grant, Kathryn Flynn, Geraldine McAuley and Amanda Murray.

Tony McCullagh, Irish Independent and past Editor of The Dublin People and Brian O'Loughlin of The Westmeath Examiner for your unwavering support.

Inklings Writing Group ran by my first ever editor, Brian McLoughlin. Your genius and creativity are unparalleled.

The Annebrook Hotel for allowing Inklings take over their library every Tuesday morning.

Susan Maguire for the last four years of writing support.

Mullingar Toastmasters and the Our New Ears committees.

Carol Sundara, Sharon O'Reilly and Martha Fitzpatrick for their advice.

Claire and all my friends in Swords.

To the best friends in the world and to all on Facebook who encouraged me to write, you have no idea how much it meant.

Most importantly to my family. Mam, Dad, Catharina and her crew. To my children Eva, Ben and Anna and the man I met 25 years ago in a bar in Vermont, my husband Brendan, who keeps me laughing.

Finally, to you the reader. Of all the books in all the world, you chose this one and I am so grateful you did. I love to chat with readers on Twitter (@MurphyLorr) so please come over and say hi.

If you could leave a review of *Into The Woods* on Amazon and Goodreads, I would be so grateful. It helps smashing readers like you find the book.

Go raibh mile maith agat. (Thanks a million)

ABOUT THE AUTHOR

Lorraine Murphy takes everyday situations and twists them into terrifying tales. She is the author of Into the Woods and numerous published, and winning, flash fiction stories.

A software engineer by profession, she's had many careers including slimming club leader, adult educator, charity co-founder, chairperson, activist and entrepreneur. As a teenager, she adored Stephen King and later found herself on the jury of an infamous murder trial.

When she's not writing, Lorraine is always into something, whether it be competing in/ for her local Toastmasters club or jumping out of a fully functional airplane. She lives in Westmeath, Ireland with her husband Brendan and three taller children.

www.lorraineamurphy.com

Printed in Great Britain
by Amazon

84731826R00144